Cover Copy

There can be only one…for both of them.

Cherub, the faerie king's daughter is one of the few who holds the ability to open a portal and travel through time. As a time-walker, she's responsible for ensuring those of her fae-blooded kind living on Earth find their soul bound match, no matter what time they might live in. The last thing she expects though is for her shifter mate to travel into the past and begin closing in on her. Her destiny is set, to aid others in finding their chosen ones, not in becoming the very one she hunts.

Highland warrior shifter Kirk Matheson won't rest until he finds the one woman who is meant to be his. Only when he discovers his mate has no wish to give up her duty in aiding her kind, does he decide the hunter must now become the hunted.

Determined in his mission to capture his elusive imp, he must find a way for them to be together…to bind the mischievous Fae Angel of Love to his side and ensure she accepts her greatest destiny, that of being his one and all.

Books by Joanne Wadsworth

The Matheson Brothers Series

Highlander's Desire, Book One
Highlander's Passion, Book Two
Highlander's Seduction, Book Three
Highlander's Kiss, Book Four
Highlander's Heart, Book Five
Highlander's Sword, Book Six
Highlander's Bride, Book Seven
Highlander's Caress, Book Eight
Highlander's Touch, Book Nine
Highlander's Shifter, Book Ten
Highlander's Claim, Book Eleven
Highlander's Courage, Book Twelve
Highlander's Mermaid, Book Thirteen

Highlander Heat Series

Highlander's Castle, Book One
Highlander's Magic, Book Two
Highlander's Charm, Book Three
Highlander's Guardian, Book Four
Highlander's Faerie, Book Five
Highlander's Champion, Book Six
Highlander's Captive (Short Story)

Billionaire Bodyguards Series

Billionaire Bodyguard Attraction, Book One
Billionaire Bodyguard Boss, Book Two
Billionaire Bodyguard Fling, Book Three

Books by Joanne Wadsworth

Regency Brides Series
The Duke's Bride, Book One
The Earl's Bride, Book Two
The Wartime Bride, Book Three
The Earl's Secret Bride, Book Four
The Prince's Bride, Book Five
Her Pirate Prince, Book Six

Princesses of Myth Series
Protector, Book One
Warrior, Book Two
Hunter (Short Story - Included in Warrior, Book Two)
Enchanter, Book Three
Healer, Book Four
Chaser, Book Five

Highlander's Seduction

The Matheson Brothers, Book Three

JOANNE WADSWORTH

Highlander's Seduction
ISBN-13: 978-1-99-003433-6
Copyright © 2015, Joanne Wadsworth
Cover Art by Joanne Wadsworth
First electronic publication: July 2015

Joanne Wadsworth
http://www.joannewadsworth.com

AUTHOR'S NOTE:
This book is a work of fiction. The names, characters, places, and incidents are products of the writer's imagination or have been used fictitiously and are not to be construed as real. Any resemblance to persons, living or dead, actual events, locale or organizations is entirely coincidental. The author does not have any control over and does not assume any responsibility for third-party websites or their content.

Published in the United States of America

First digital publication: July 2015
First print publication: September 2015

Acknowledgements

I have an incredibly supportive family who allow me so much time to write. Huge thanks go to my hubby, Jason, and kiddies, Marisa, Caleb, Cruise and Rocco. Hugs.

For my readers, I can't thank you enough for joining me, and taking this journey to where imagination and magic soar.

Gilleoin – The Legend

In the twelfth century, a man named Gilleoin became the first and only known man to hold bear shifter blood, an ability gifted to him by The Most High One. His clan was called Matheson, and when he mated with a woman carrying faerie blood, they created a line shrouded in secrecy, a line that far into the future, now neared extinction…

The Seer – Nessa

The ancient House of Clan Matheson, led by Gilleoin, the Chief of Clan Matheson, Scotland, 1210.

Restless and on edge, Nessa strode down the winding stairs from her chamber and entered the great hall. The large vaulted room held a sweeping crown of wooden beamed rafters that rose to an impressive height and within it a hundred or more warriors attired in their clan plaids, clanked tankards of ale together. Lively chatter bubbled forth as her kin feasted on their evening meal. All appeared as it should be, yet still her worry only increased.

She slowed next to the wide arched stone fireplace where sparks flared and firelight shimmered across the hefty clan shield hanging over it. With one finger, she traced along the silver edge where rubies, sapphires and emeralds shone. The jewels surrounded their clan's crest stamped in the center, an image depicting two bears as supporters either side of their chief's arms. Those bears signified what they all fought for—the survival of a loyal race of bear shifters—Gilleoin's line. He was the first, gifted with his ability to shift by The Most High One, and now his twin sons had become the second generation of shifters.

Over twenty years ago when Gilleoin's sons were born, she'd first spoken the prophecy which would be handed down through the generations, a prophecy that had been unveiled far into the future and with it had brought the recent arrival of travelers from the twenty-first century. Those travelers, three identical warrior brothers of immense strength were known as the 'power of three.' Iain, Finlay, and Kirk could shift shape into the form of the bear, draw claws and roar as Gilleoin and his sons could. Along with them had come Iain's mate, Isla, a woman of dual shifter-fae blood, the daughter of Murdock, her clan's chief and seer.

Even over the wide chasm of centuries separating them, Nessa had come to know Murdock through joint visions and considered him a dear friend. Their beliefs and goals for their people matched, although unfortunately in the future where Murdock lived, Gilleoin's shifter clan now neared extinction and required a new infusion of fae blood within their shifter line if they wished to survive. That infusion was one both she and Murdock intended to see come to fruition, and now with the 'power of three' here in the past, they'd made a start.

At the dais Kirk sat, the youngest of the three warrior brothers, his gaze firm on the tall stained glass window and the setting sun beyond that hovered on the horizon. In the weeks since the three brothers had arrived, Finlay had found Arabel, his chosen one, and joined with her. Now 'twas Kirk's time. He awaited the coming of tonight's full moon to guide him. This was the one night of the month when his shifter senses would lead him directly to her, when his mate would no longer remain beyond his touch or sight.

Kirk clenched his fists as his restlessness mounted. For five long years he'd been searching for his mate but had never found her, not when she resided beyond his future time and instead right here in the past.

As the sun dipped lower, the skies darkened and a quietness suddenly settled over all within the hall.

The full moon rose and Kirk stood, his eyes closed and his breathing slow as if he settled himself.

Nessa closed her eyes too as the magnitude of the moment rolled through her. As a seer, she'd been gifted with a skill she upheld to the best of her ability, to ensure her clan never faltered, and so too she'd look after Kirk and ensure he found his mate just as his brothers had. She wouldn't fail the 'power of three,' just as they hadn't failed her or their kin here during the recent battle to save the fae village farther along the loch. Because of the 'power of three,' hope now bloomed for their clan as never before.

Images fluttered at the periphery of her mind and a vision flickered into life. A young woman stood at the edge of the fae village's pebbly shore, her white fur cloak wrapped firmly around her. 'Twas Cherub, the faerie king's daughter. She'd never mistake her. Cherub was a close friend and a fae time-walker who was able to cloak her true form and become as one with the very *air* itself by taking on a mist form. Cherub could also sense when two were mated and 'twas her duty to bring those two together. That duty had been one she'd upheld for over a thousand years and across a wide divide of centuries. She was an immortal with flawless skin that sparkled like that of the stars she moved amongst.

Carefully, Nessa focused on Cherub as the lass raised her arms and allowed the wind to bring to her the secrets she needed to unravel. The wind rushed all around Cherub and the fae princess frowned and shook her head as if suddenly confused.

From time to time, Nessa could connect to Cherub when under the weight of a vision and in so doing they could speak to each other. Cherub was one of the few who she talked with in such a way, Murdock the other. She opened up her mind and spoke to Cherub. *"What is wrong, my dear? A vision has shown me you, although I know no' why."*

"Nessa, something is amiss. 'Tis to do with Kirk. I sense who he is mated to, and even though I've always known his mate was fae, this is the first time I've ever sensed exactly who she is."

"And who is his mated one?"

At the dais, a commotion sounded and Nessa opened her eyes.

"I sense her." Kirk pumped a fist into the air, his golden gaze flashing with fierce determination. "She's at the village." Firm words and all within the great hall cheered.

Nessa's vision swirled again and she returned to Cherub. *"Kirk senses his mate."*

"I dinnae know what to do." Cherub paced the beach, her long golden locks swaying about her waist. *"Nessa, I must ask a favor of you. Is it possible for you to keep Kirk from leaving the keep this eve? I need more time."*

"No one can halt a shifter from seeking out his mate, no' even I. Who is his chosen one?"

"Me." A shuddering breath left her lips. *"What am I to do? I cannae take a mate, no' when my duty to my people must come first. They need me, and I cannae forsake them now, no' in these most urgent of times."*

"If you and Kirk are soul bound, then you are each other's match in every way. No matter what your duty is, he is still your destiny."

"Kirk is only one amongst the many who I need to care for." A quiet look of longing crossed Cherub's face. *"I cannae choose him over all others. Look at what happened to Amelia. She is a time-walker and when she took a mate, she gave up her duty. That is something I cannae do."*

"Then what is your intention?"

"I will need to forego the bond, which will be downright difficult. Wish me luck, Nessa. I shall need it." Cherub straightened her shoulders and blew her a kiss. *"We will speak*

again soon."

"We shall, although it isnae luck you need, my dear, but to no' forget the depth of the mated bond. There can be only one...for both of you." Nessa blew her a kiss in return and opened her eyes.

Surely the Fae Angel of Love wouldn't be able to turn her mate away. Cherub was the very woman who hunted those who were soul bound and brought them together.

Kirk marched past her and flew out the door. Naught would stop him until he'd found his chosen one. He was a hunter of the most driven sort, which meant now Cherub had become the hunted. Aye, she'd need to keep a close eye on Cherub and Kirk over the coming days. Never would she allow Gilleoin's future line to fall into extinction. The 'power of three' needed to ring with their greatest strength, and for that to occur, all three brothers had to find their mates and complete the bond. Kirk was the last, although not the least.

The Seer – Murdock Matheson

Matheson Castle, led by Murdock Matheson, the Chief of Clan Matheson, a man with dual shifter-fae blood, Scotland, current day.

Murdock Matheson paced the water's edge of Loch Alsh, his current frustration riding him hard. It had been days since his last vision and he detested not seeing his daughter, Isla, and the three warrior brothers known as the 'power of three,' who'd traveled with her over eight-hundred years into the past.

Mere days ago, the 'power of three' along with their mates had successfully saved the fae village from the MacKenzie chief's attack and now their shifter clan held more hope for their future than ever before.

If only he could force a vision. At least Nessa, the seer of ancient times, would be watching over his kin. Of that he had no doubt.

"Chief!" Daniel, his right hand man, jogged along the grassy verge of the loch's shoreline, the castle's fortified stone walls rising high behind him. The thick slabs of gray stone were bathed a glorious golden hue as the sun dipped below the horizon and the moon rose majestically overhead.

"Is all well?"

"More than well." Hands on his hips, Daniel halted and grinned. "Several of our unmated men have reported their senses are stirring as never before. They're certain their chosen ones now await them, although they need to leave tonight and begin their search."

"Inform them that they may and that I wish them well. Certainly if their searches lead them this night to a place where no one awaits them, then it could well mean their mates reside in the past as Finlay and Kirk's mates do. We will need Cherub if that is so." Murdock rarely spoke of Cherub, keeping her secrets as needed. He clapped Daniel on the back. "Ensure all those who need to leave on their search have all they require at hand. This is our time, for our clan to embrace a new future."

"Will do, Chief, and it's a new future we long for." Daniel grasped Murdock's forearm in a firm warrior hold then jogged back toward the keep in his clan plaid.

Aye, a new time had now dawned for their shifter line, one of renewed hope and endless possibilities.

Quietly, he closed his eyes and focused on Nessa.

He couldn't force a vision, but with this level of worry and need consuming him, surely one was close to rising. He'd remain alert if one—

A flurry of images swirled to blazing life and he grasped ahold of them. Nessa stood within the great hall of the ancient House of Clan Matheson in an elegant olive gown, her head bowed under the weight of a vision as her clansmen partook of their evening meal around her. He tapped into her mind and followed the path of her vision.

At the fae village along the loch, a young woman wearing a white fur cloak stood on the pebbly beach. Cherub. He touched his heart. Cherub had visited him from time to time over the years, the very first during his darkest days, not long after he'd lost his wife to cancer only a week following Isla's birth. Lost in his grief, he'd barely been able to care for himself let alone his newborn daughter. Yet he'd promised his wife on her passing that he'd raise their child with all the love and devotion she would have done, a promise he'd kept and would continue to do so.

Cherub had been the one to console him, to assure him his wife awaited him in the land of the fae beyond the veil, in a place that for now would remain beyond his reach, but not forever. One day he would join her, when his time on Earth was done.

"*Murdock?*" Nessa's voice reverberated softly through his mind.

"*I'm here, my friend. How is Isla?*"

"*Your daughter is very well. Iain keeps a close watch over her, as do I. She misses you.*"

"*As I miss her. Tell her I love her. I saw Cherub. She looks troubled.*"

"*She's discovered this eve that she is mated to Kirk, a bond she feels she cannae allow to take due to her duty.*"

Cherub was devoted to those of fae blood who walked this Earth. She ensured each and every one of her people found their soul bound mate, even though they might be separated by a divide of time. She could command the very *air* itself and open portals in time. He drew his focus back to the young woman who held a special place in his heart and always would. Just as he could communicate with Nessa during a vision, so too he could do so with Cherub when his sight led him to her. "*Cherub, how are you?*"

"*I am well, Murdock.*" A smile lifted Cherub's lips. "*How are you?*"

"*I have good news. Several of my men have just reported sensing their mates, for the first time.*"

"*Many of them shall be led to a place this eve where their mate should be, but they willnae find who they search for. No' when their mates reside here in this time. The same will have occurred for the other shifter clan farther across the Highlands. I need you to speak to their chief, Michael. Let him know the Fae Angel of Love's duty stands firm and always shall.*"

"I'll inform him. Michael's been eager to hear more news about Iain, Finlay and Kirk. He misses his sons and will be pleased to hear of your bond taking form with Kirk."

"*I'm afraid I cannae accept the bond with my mate, no' if I wish to aid all those who will soon need me. Kirk is but one of many.*"

"*No one has ever been able to defy the mated bond.*"

"*Then I shall attempt to be the first.*"

"*There is no need for you to deny what should be.*"

"*There is every need if I'm to continue to care for my people.*" Warmth radiated from her through their link and enveloped him. "*We shall speak again soon. Your clan shall need me in the coming days and I willnae forsake you, or them. Of that I give you my word.*"

"*Then take care, my friend, for I too shall be watching over you.*"

"*Until the next time.*" Cherub's image fluttered away, as did his vision and his connection to Nessa.

The fae time-walker was devoted to each and every one of her people, her work usually done in secret. He only hoped she was as devoted to caring for herself as well. There was strength in allowing the mated bond and joining with the one who was always meant to be theirs. Aye, a mated pair should never be separated, not even when duty stood in their way.

Chapter 1

At the fae village, farther along the loch from the ancient House of Clan Matheson, Scotland, 1210.

Under a darkening sky, Cherub paced the pebbly beach before the fae village, the wind whistling around her. It flapped her white fur cloak back from her shoulders and whipped her blond hair in a frenzy. High above, the full moon rose and bathed the Earth in its heavenly glow. This one night of the month always offered such promise to those who were mated, yet this eve, it brought only longing to her very soul, a longing that would soon be crushed. She couldn't forsake her fae-blooded kind, not when so many would now need her aid in seeking out their mated one.

"Papa!" A lad dashed through the gate in the high stone wall surrounding the village and raced toward the foaming water's edge. 'Twas Joseph, Amelia's son. Wearing loose-legged tan breeches two inches too short on his legs and a long green tunic, Joseph swung a wooden pail in his hand as he hurried along the grassy trail.

Ten years ago, Amelia, the second of only three time-walkers born to their people, had traveled from the future to the past and become soul bound to Olaf here in this time. When their bond had taken form, her friend had chosen to forego her skill and devote herself to her mate. That had left Cherub as the only one to care for their Earthbound fae, the third time-walker caring for those beyond the veil. Still, 'twas a duty Cherub adored and one she'd never forsake.

"Wait there, Joseph." Beyond the choppy breakers, Olaf waved from his skiff then hauled his nets in. He rowed into shore, bounded out and roped his boat to a boulder. Joseph handed him the pail and Olaf filled it with his catch before the two of them walked back along the beach toward her. With a smile, Olaf stopped and gazed at her. "How are you this eve, Cherub?"

"I'm very well. How is Amelia?"

"A little anxious following the recent battle on these shores. 'Tis good to see you're back."

"I can never stay away from my kin here for long." Thankfully she'd only been gone a short time. Bending, she rustled Joseph's windblown brown locks. "Tell your mama I shall visit her soon, now that I've returned to this time."

"I will." Joseph ogled her sparkly skin. "Mama said she saw your papa beyond the veil, and more than once when she traveled there. She said the king's skin glitters too."

"Aye, his does. Each eldest child born within the royal line holds such sparkly skin as mine." She was one of seven, the eldest of all her siblings. She kissed Joseph's cheek. His mother was like a sister to her, and Joseph was the first and only child born to a time-walker. Like his mother, he too would be an immortal, his soul having been blood bound to Amelia's through his birth.

Olaf wrapped an arm around Joseph's shoulder. "I've caught plenty of fish this eve, Cherub. Are you able to join us for the evening meal?"

"I wish I could, but there is a man I must wait here to meet.

My thanks though for your kind invitation."

"Then you must come as soon as you can. Amelia misses you."

"As I miss her. Tell her I shall visit on the morrow."

"I will. Take care." Olaf squeezed her arm then led Joseph up the trail and through the gate into the village. Amelia and her kin were so happy here, and she too couldn't have been happier for them. Joseph was a treasure, a child who brought such delight to one and all who met him.

With a soft sigh, she turned her gaze back toward Matheson House. This coming encounter was one that tore at her. She was to meet her soul bound mate and then turn him away. Life wasn't fair, but then that she'd learnt well over the centuries.

Down the trail toward the sea-gate landing, a warrior with midnight black locks brushing his shoulders ran. He bounded aboard a skiff, released the mooring rope then coiled and stored it under the center seat. With the oars in hand, he rowed.

Once he cleared the bay, he tucked his oars away and raised the sail. The wind filled it with a hearty slap and with his feet braced wide along one side and the ropes in hand, he steered the skiff as it shot off like an arrow toward her.

Her fae senses reached out toward his and butterflies abounded in her belly. Kirk's drive to reach the village was honed completely in on her, the one woman who was meant to be his, and the one woman she intended to deny him of. Finding his chosen one had consumed him these past five years, just as it had his two identical brothers who'd now found their mates. Although never once had she known that 'twas her Kirk searched for. If only she had, then she could have let him down far sooner and thus allowed him to move on and enjoy his life.

The wind plastered Kirk's billowy white tunic against his muscled chest and sent the sword holstered at his side swaying. He would be here within a minute or two and there was naught more she could do now but anxiously await his arrival.

Over her shoulder, the need of those within the houses of stone and clay cloistered so tightly together called out to her and touched her very heart. Throughout the days and years to come, so many would need her aid and that knowledge firmed her stance. Their people couldn't lose another time-walker, a fact she hoped her mate could accept.

With her decision made, she dissolved into a mist and became as one with the very air itself, the element she commanded. 'Twas best Kirk not have her image in his mind. If he did, then that would make their parting all the more harder.

Kirk steered his skiff toward land, lowered the sail as he neared the shore and jumped into the knee-deep water. He hauled his boat onto the beach and in snug black leather pants, marched toward her. He strode past her then stopped and swung about. With a determined slash to his lips and his nose to the air, he breathed deep and prowled back. In a wide circle, he moved, each of his steps drawing him closer and closer to her unseen position.

"Why can't I see you, my elusive imp? I'm finally here in the right time and place and I should be able to." He halted directly in front of her, lifted one hand and swept it in a wide arc.

His hand passed right through her, and her very soul shimmered with need.

"Where are you?" he whispered into the wind, raw pain in his voice.

Her heart ached with what could never be. A soul bound match was what she sought for others, believed in to the greatest degree. "I'm so sorry, Kirk. You have my sincerest apologies for withholding myself from you." She allowed her voice to flow to him. Leaving him wondering about her wasn't something she'd ever be able to do, not to the man her very soul had now been bound to. "You and I, and this mated bond that has formed between us, it cannae be."

"You know my name?" He searched where she stood.

"I do, and that is because 'tis now emblazoned on my heart."

"Why can't I see you?"

"I'm a time-walker, one of only three who can command the very air itself. 'Tis my element and if I wish, so too I can become as one with it."

"Why would you withhold yourself from me?"

"I…" She wavered in her stance and took form, although she remained fully cloaked and unseen. "You can touch me now if you wish."

He swept one hand out, his fingers sliding through her locks then slowly, he brought his hand to his chest, his fist clenched around a long strand of her pale blond hair. "Thank you."

"My name is Cherub. I am also the one who hears the whispers between souls who arena yet aligned so that I might bring them together across time, no matter where they might be."

"You're the Fae Angel of Love?" Surprise widened his eyes. "I've heard of you, or I should say the legend. Tales spoken of the Fae Angel of Love give our clan hope."

"I'm more than just a tale. I was born to serve my people and have done so for over a thousand years." She looked into his eyes and almost drowned in his stunning golden gaze. A shifter's eyes, although there was more. They were rimmed with a glimmer of starburst yellow, adding a spark of heat that sent another bout of butterflies flittering about in her belly. "So many seek my aid, and my duty is to those of fae blood who walk this Earth."

"I'm one of Ivan's direct descendants, Gilleoin's second-born son, and unlike Gilleoin's firstborn line, our clan is shifter alone. I have no fae blood."

"Aye, 'tis true your clan does no' hold any fae skills as the firstborn son's line does, yet Sorcha's blood still flows through your line all the same." Sorcha, Gilleoin's wife and Nessa's daughter was a strongly skilled fae who held the ability of aura reading. "That trace of fae blood, although diluted over the centuries, is still enough to call to me." She cupped his cheek, her lips lifting. "I have spoken to Isla's father, Murdock, this night and he has informed me that many of the unmated men in his clan now sense their chosen ones. The same will have occurred for your clan farther across the Highlands from him. I also asked him to speak to your father and to let Michael know I will watch over one and all, just as I've always done."

"As I intend to now watch over you." He slid his hand gently over hers and closed his eyes. "I want my mate, the one woman who was always meant to mine. I want you, Cherub. Please, show yourself fully to me. Uncloak."

His demand to see her tugged at her heart and caused her to sway toward him, to falter for a mere moment in her stance. She should walk away from him now, and before any ties between their souls began to weave together.

"I'm sorry. That I cannae do."

"Legend says the Fae Angel of Love is the faerie king's firstborn child."

"Aye, I am." She stroked her fingers back and forth over his skin. Touching him, even for this stolen moment in time, soothed her very soul. "You must understand, there is too much at stake for me to allow our joining. So many others need me."

"As I now need you too. Surely you can take one night off from your duties. Aren't you curious at all about who I am and why a bond has taken between us? Give me some time." He smoothed his hand over her wrist and up her arm then slid his fingers under her hair and around her nape. "I'm so incredibly curious about you. I've wondered for five long years just who you were, as well as craved the thought of getting to know you. You can't leave me now."

She should move away, yet his hold, so deliciously tender, and the sheer look of desire in his gaze even though he couldn't see her kept her rooted to the spot. "I've never once sensed I was bound to another. Five years may have passed for you, but for me, only a few minutes have."

"I see." He found her other arm then swept down to her hand and threaded their fingers together. "I understand your dilemma. I certainly don't wish to see my fellow kin lose the chance of being brought to their mated one. Holding hope is all that the men in our shifter line hold onto, and now I've found you, I too have no intention of losing that hope. There must be a way around all of this, so that both of us can receive what we need to from our bond."

"My duty is all-consuming, barely allowing me any time for myself, let alone a mate."

"Then allow me to aid you. I needn't be a burden but a partner to share the load." Slowly, he lowered to one knee, brought her hand to his lips and pressed a soft kiss against her palm. "Cherub, from this day forth, I give you my oath. All I desire is to keep you safe, to honor your needs above my own. Allow me to stand at your side, to aid you in your duty. I'll do all I can to ensure you never falter in caring for your people."

A slow heat invaded her limbs and spread in a rippling wave through her body. His words touched her heart. "You shouldnae have made such a vow to me."

"My word is absolute and I won't take it back. Meeting you is all I've ever dreamed of, and the thought of you leaving me because your duty is so all-consuming tears my very soul in two. Give me a chance. Allow me to prove I speak the truth and will never fail you." He rose to his feet, scooped her into his arms and walked with her toward the forest rising high behind the village. The tops of the pine trees swayed in the breeze and an owl hooted from deep within.

"Where are you taking me?" She looped her arms around his neck and held on as he strode along the trail into the darkening forest.

"There is a special place not far from here, one I discovered not long after my arrival. I'd like to take you there. Give me this one night. Don't leave me or forego our bond until you've given me the chance to prove my vow was spoken in truth. I would forever honor it, and you."

Goodness. If she granted his request and spent one night with him, would she then be able to walk away from him once the sun had risen in the morning? Soul bound mates would do anything for each other. That she'd witnessed time and time again over the centuries, although Amelia had still stood down from her duty after accepting the bond with Olaf. That she couldn't allow to have happen to her.

"You've gone very quiet all of a sudden. Does that mean you agree to one night?"

He asked for so little and right now no other needed her. "I'll give you one night, although no more."

"Thank you." He buried his nose in her hair and grinning, drew in a deep breath. "Mmm, you smell delicious, like fresh air and an ocean breeze. Where do you live, Cherub?"

"My place is here on Earth, amongst those of fae blood, wherever that might be and whatever century that draws me to." In truth, she owned several parcels of land, had built a home on one such plot and favored it as a home base. She also kept a chamber right here at Matheson House, one Nessa insisted she use as often as she needed to, which would be greatly needed during the coming days and weeks ahead now so many shifters in the future would be seeking their mates here in this time. "You can put me down if you wish. I've agreed to one night and I'll gladly walk with you."

"Thanks for the offer but I'd rather hold onto you." He strode along a leaf-strewn path, the canopy high and thick above and blocking all sign of the moon. "You feel so good in my arms."

"Do you carry women about often?" He was rather adept at it.

"No." He chuckled. "You are and will be the only woman I'll ever hold close to my heart. That I promise you. So too my bear is also feeling restless this eve and demands this touch. Releasing you right now would be impossible."

"'Tis a shame I willnae get to meet your bear. Is his pelt the same color as your hair?" His black locks were as dark as a midnight sky.

"I'll show you my bear, if you uncloak and show me your true form. Shall we make a deal?"

"Nay, no deal." It appeared her mate liked to negotiate.

"Do you hear that?" Kirk cocked one ear.

Up ahead, the sea crashed against the high cliffs and the sound traveled to her. Kirk was taking her toward the isolated bay farther along the inner channel of the loch, one of the few places she too adored. "I do." She touched his jaw and turned his gaze from the trail to hers. His golden eyes glinted in the dark. "We are headed to one of my favorite places."

"I wish I could see you." He searched her gaze. "What color are your eyes, my mate?"

"They're blue, a very plain and dull blue."

"There is no shade of blue that is plain or dull." A low branch loomed and he ducked his head, his lips brushing her cheek as he kept her from scraping against it as well. "I can feel you're clothed in a fur cape. What else do you wear?"

She grasped the edges of her fluttering cloak and tucked the fur tighter about her. "Just clothes."

"You're so elusive. Come on. You must give me a hint. He nuzzled her neck, his nose buried deep in her hair. "I'll forever wonder otherwise."

"They're clothes which keep me warm no matter where I might travel." She touched a finger to his lower lip and swept to one raised corner then back again to the center. He had such soft lips, and when his tongue darted out and he licked her finger, she gasped.

"Mmm, I see you're elusive and tasty." He strode uphill, stepped over a fallen log barring their way and along the winding trail toward the cliff top that overlooked the bay.

She tucked her head into his shoulder and rubbed her cheek against the thin white cotton of his tunic. The deep V collar was loosely laced and she slipped her hand inside his shirt and stroked his golden skin. The need to touch one's mate was natural and she didn't fight that desire. So too she'd agreed to one night, so she may as well allow herself this moment of release. "You feel warm, almost too warm."

"That's because my shifter blood runs hotter than most, and right now it's been a couple of days since I last shifted. Heat builds to a higher degree when I'm overdue for the Change." He emerged at the top of the cliff overlooking the curve of the bay below. Moonlight glimmered across the white-capped waves rolling onto the white sand beach, turning them a stunning silvery hue.

This bay held a touch of magic, was only accessible by a tunnel in the cliff at the base. Few knew of the hidden entrance, which ensured this protected place remained so very private and pristine.

"You said before you're one of only three who holds command over the element of air. Where are the other two time-walkers located?"

"Jeremiah's duty is to the full-blooded fae beyond the veil. He rarely has time to aid me on Earth. The last is Amelia, one of my dearest friends. We are close, like sisters in truth."

"Where does Amelia's duty lie, here or beyond the veil?" With care, he traversed the edge of the cliff where it led downward toward the secret entrance. On one side, the odd stone rattled loose under his feet and clacked down the side of the sheer rock wall, while on the other, the rough branches of the swaying pine trees brushed his arms.

"Amelia used to aid me here on Earth, but she stood down

from her duty ten years ago when she became soul bound with Olaf. They live at the village and have a son named Joseph. He's the first child to be born to a time-walker and such a delight. He also holds the skill of foreknowledge, an ability similar to a seer's although still a little different."

"I've not met Amelia or Olaf. Is she too an immortal as you are?" He reached the base of the cliff, lowered her to her feet and with their fingers twined together, brushed aside a clump of trailing ivy covering the slim opening in the rock wall. Keeping ahold of her, he edged through the thin gap and weaved along the dark tunnel.

"She is. Amelia's mate is also an immortal, as is their child."

"How is Olaf an immortal?"

"A time-walker, once they take a mate, can hold their chosen one's soul to theirs. Amelia spoke a spell which bound a piece of Olaf's soul to hers, so like her, he too will never sicken or age. They will walk the same path for the rest of their lives, together as one."

"That's a beautiful thing."

"It is." They reached the end of the tunnel and emerged before the beach. She jumped free onto the soft sand and twirled around, her feet digging in deep. This secluded bay with its thin strip of white sand always took her breath away.

"Cherub?" Kirk swept his hands through the air as he searched for her. "Where are you?"

"I'm right here." She twirled around again. "I love this place."

"As soon as I stumbled upon it, I felt as if I'd come home. There's a secluded bay very similar to this one at Loch Shin, a place I'm often drawn to, and a place that's only a few hours' drive from my home at Ivanson Castle." He glanced at the sand she'd kicked up then followed her movement and caught her in his arms. His hands slid underneath the flapping sides of her cloak and around her back. Caressing her, he swept down her sides and over her waist. A grin lifted his lips. "You're wearing a silk gown. What color?"

"The gown is white, as is my cape. 'Tis one of my favorite colors. Have you truly been drawn to Loch Shin?" She raised her hands to the glittering jewel of the darkened sky above and leaned back, allowing him to take her full weight as she did.

"During these past five years my search for you has only ever led me in and around that area, more times than not to a place called Angel Bay along the loch's shores. Is that place special to you at all?"

"Oh my." The home she'd built and considered a base rested high on the cliffs overlooking Angel Bay.

"Is that an aye?" He sank to the sand and took her with him as he laid down.

"I—I—" Speaking a mistruth to him tore at her. Instead, she tucked one errant lock of his hair behind his ear and said, "I enjoy visiting Angel Bay, just as I enjoy visiting this place. Both bring me comfort, as well as allow me to walk the shoreline in complete seclusion."

"Hmm, why do I feel as if you're not quite telling me the whole truth?" He removed his sword belt, set it beside him then with his warm hands on her hips, brought her back against him. Gently, he smoothed one hand along her outer thigh then tucked her top leg snugly between his leather-clad legs, their bodies in complete alignment from head to toe. She wasn't surprised by his move, or his need to hold her close. Those who were soul bound required touch on a deeper level to most. He skimmed up her arm and swept one finger along her gown's low-cut neckline. "Can you explain a little more?"

"Nay, I dinnae wish to encourage your pursuit and explaining more will do so."

"Ha." He chuckled. "You're my mate, the one woman I will always pursue, and there is nothing you can say or do to cease that encouragement." He caught her cheeks in his hands and traced his thumbs under her eyes and over her nose. He smoothed along her jaw, over her chin then slowly delved across her lips. His breath stuttered and he leaned in, pressed his forehead against hers. "You have the smoothest, softest skin."

"I have no' aged past my twentieth year even though I've lived over a thousand years." A gentle sea breeze whispered around them, lifted his shirt hem and gave her a glimpse of his tanned abs. His black pants hung low on his hips and the leather clung to his powerful thighs. She lifted her gaze back to his and almost drowned in the deep desire reflecting back at her. She palmed his chest, his heart thundering under her hand. A simple walk was leading to so much more—more she couldn't currently turn away from.

"Cherub, I wish for a kiss. Would that be permissible?"

"I dinnae think—"

"Thinking is currently not permitted." He lowered his mouth to her, his lips so aching soft as he joined them together, then he deepened their kiss and licked her tongue, his breath mingling seductively with hers.

Aye, thinking shouldn't be permitted. Why not live in the moment, even if only for one night? Granting herself at least that much, settled her deep inside. Gently, she sucked his lower lip into her mouth then indulged in her need for more. She kissed him, deeply, then grasped his shoulders and pulled him fully on top of her, his heavenly weight exactly what she needed. She melted into the sand, reveling in his warm spicy scent as it surrounded and embedded itself into her. "I like your kisses, Kirk."

"I'm sure I could convince you to like a whole lot more of me if you were only open to the possibility."

"I also like your intriguing mind." She kissed him again and he kissed her back. In all the centuries that had passed her by, never had she taken one stolen moment like this and kept it all to herself. Being with him right now was all she desired.

"This could get rather addictive, rather fast." He lifted his head and grinned at her, and she grinned right back, not that he could see her smile. "Don't you think so, my elusive imp?"

"Very addictive and also very wrong." She sank her hands into his hair and raked her nails lightly across his scalp. "Kirk, I dinnae wish for you to live a lonely life, so should you wish to join with another—I mean—you shouldnae miss out on all life has to offer just because your soul was bound to the wrong woman."

"You are the perfect woman for me, and I've already given you my vow. I will not forsake it." He rubbed his nose against hers. "You also need to give me something to hold onto, to keep my hope alive, that you might one day change your mind. Give me your promise in return, Cherub, that you'll at least consider allowing our bond to take."

"I cannae." She shook her head, and he pressed his palms to her cheeks and followed her movement.

"I see. You're going to be a stubborn mate."

"I am not a stubborn mate but a wise one." She palmed the back of his head and brought his mouth back to within a breath of hers. "I also wish for another kiss."

"So do I. Of at least that we're in complete agreement on." He swooped in and kissed her, taking her breath away with his passion. He was a seduction she desired more of and she couldn't help but give into her current need. Living a thousand years alone hadn't been easy. 'Twas time to give into her destiny, even if only for this one night.

* * * *

Kirk kissed Cherub with all the longing he'd held deep inside him these past five years. He caressed her sides, roamed down and gripped her hips. He rolled them both until she came up on top of him, her cape sweeping his sides and her hood falling softly over her head. Within the cocoon of fur, he caught a glimmer of her features, one delicate earlobe, the partial sight dazzling and making him blink. Did her skin sparkle? Or was that just his imagination? Hell, he longed to see more of her, to have her fully uncloak herself, but so too he also understood her desire not to. She worried that in allowing their mated bond to take form, her calling to bring those who were soul bound together would no longer take precedence. Only she didn't know him. He'd do all he could to aid her. Never would he hold her back from her duty.

"Mmm, Kirk." She murmured his name against his lips then kissed him again, so deeply and completely he fell into her silken web. Nowhere else did he desire to be other than right here with her. She scattered each and every one of his thoughts, so swiftly and decisively. All that roared through his mind was the need to mate, to mark his chosen one and to never let her go.

"I need more, Cherub."

"I cannae allow a joining."

"I understand, but surely you can allow me to see to your needs and mine, or at least to take the edge of this hunger riding us." The front tie of her cape tickled his neck and he groped for the elusive ribbon, tugged it loose and pushed her cloak from her. As soon as the fur left her body, it became exposed to his sight in the moonlight. Eyes closed, he used every one of his bear's senses to its fullest extent to memorize what he could of her. Her scent, fresher than the air itself, embedded itself deeply within him. He wanted to smother her in his own scent, to ensure all who came near her knew she belonged to him. Nuzzling her neck, he licked over her thumping pulse. The deep desire to bite her as his shifter kind did raced through his blood until it became an unstoppable beat.

One night. She'd promised him this one night, and he intended to make it the most memorable one she'd ever known. Following that, he'd continue to convince her of his pure intentions.

A low rumble vibrated in his chest as he pressed himself against her and sucked on her offered skin. She was all woman, and all his. "I need to bite you, and for you to bite me in return. Mark me as yours, Cherub."

"It will mean naught."

"Not to me it won't." He palmed the back of her head and held her mouth to his neck. As he did, he licked her erratic pulse point in the same spot.

"I shouldnae be doing this, only I cannae think straight right now." She clutched his shoulders, her nails digging into his flesh then she shoved his collar to the side and exposed his skin.

"Don't think about anything, only about doing." He razzed her skin with his teeth then bit her.

"Oooh, that I like." She arched into him, then dipped her head and sank her teeth into his skin in return.

Arousal hit him hard and fast.

"More, I need more." She rocked against him and likely the same surge of desire raced through her as it did through him. Their bite wasn't just a mark of claim but also a bite that brought on fierce sexual desire.

"If I do anything you don't like, then tell me." Slowly, he eased his hand inside the fabric of her bodice, the silk sliding sensuously across the back of his hand. He palmed her full breast and thumbed her peaking nipple. He needed to taste her. Gently, he eased the fabric over her shoulder and exposed her breast. He certainly damn well wished he could see her. Swiftly, he drew the bud deep inside his mouth and played the tip with his tongue. She tasted exquisite, and as he imbibed on her, she clung to him and pushed the sweet morsel even deeper into his mouth. He couldn't halt his desire, didn't even have the chance of doing so. He freed her other breast from its silken bond and gave it as much attention as he'd laved on the first.

"Dinnae stop. Bite me again, Kirk."

"I'd love to." He nipped the upper swell of her breast as he swept upward then sucked on the sensitive skin where her shoulder and neck met. "Ready?"

"Aye, I'm beyond ready."

He bit down and she cried out, her gasp so sweet, as if she was on the brink of an orgasm. Damn it. If she was close, he intended to take her right over the edge and to the heights he desired for her to soar. Everything within him demanded he see to her every need. She'd given up her life for the care of her people, and he would do the same in a heartbeat for her as well. He rolled her onto her side, patted down her body and scrunched her gown's hem up.

Even though he'd never touched a woman before, he certainly wasn't unaware of what she'd need in order to reach the heights of ecstasy. Few would be who lived in his time. He slid his palm along her inner thigh and nudged her legs farther apart. She widened them and her heat and honey scent called to him. At the entrance to her core, he halted, his fingertips touching the soft curls guarding her most private place. "I need to touch you," he rasped. "Deep inside. May I?"

"Kissing you is clearly dangerous." Softly whispered words as the ties of his pants loosened at her invisible touch. "I've lived a long time, past, future and present included and there is little I'm unaware of that can happen between a man and a woman. I mean, I've never slept with a man, but if you touch me right now then I intend to touch you in return. I want to give you what you desire, or at least what I can for this one night."

"I desire you and whatever you need."

"And I desire the same for you, Kirk. Touch me." She wrapped her hand around his cock and he nearly exploded at her touch right then and there.

"I'm all yours. Touch me too, as you please." He eased his fingers between her folds and rubbed her slick nub. "And I mean for all time, Cherub, not just this one night. You're my mate, the only woman I'll ever touch, the only woman I'll ever desire."

Her need called to him, her sweet scent swirling seductively around him. All he wanted to do was wriggle down, flip her skirts higher and imbibe at the very heart of her. His bear fairly raged at him to do so. Instead he plunged one finger inside her hot channel and bumped his nose against hers as he tried to find her lips.

"I'm right here." She angled her head and captured his mouth and kissed him, just as ravenously as he kissed her. She was the only one who could provide him with the ultimate sustenance he needed.

Aye she was his one and all, the only woman his soul would ever seek. He stroked deep inside her then pulled out to caress her clit, his desire to give her everything she needed roaring through him.

"Oh, that feels sooo good. Dinnae stop." She worked his cock in long pulls then swiped her thumb over the head. His cock wept for more and he pushed deeper into her delicious touch.

"Your hand on me feels exquisite." He licked along her neck and laved the mark he'd given her then plunged two fingers deep inside her channel. He intended to love her however he could. He nipped her skin, dotting each and every inch under his mouth as he moved toward her breasts. Living a lifetime at her side was a dream he intended to make a reality, although clearly convincing her of the same would be a challenge, although one he was more than up for. "Cherub, tell me exactly what you want me to do."

"You're doing everything and more than I could ever ask for." She cupped his balls with one hand and with the other, she pumped his shaft. His spine tingled and a low burn hummed at the base of his spine, one that ricocheted around to the front and had him gritting his teeth to keep from coming.

"Damn it. I won't come before you." He drove his fingers into her and she whimpered and pushed her breasts against his chest.

"And I won't come afore you." She bit his neck and fire raced through his blood.

He exploded, his essence spurting from him in one fast burn. He coated her fingers and as he did, he sank his teeth into her neck and she cried out his name. Her inner core dragged his fingers in even deeper inside her and she came, over and over. He roared his pleasure. Never had he experienced such satisfaction as he had in this very moment, a satisfaction he intended to imbibe in again. Now, he just needed to convince his mate that he'd never accept another. Only her. He'd also never take her away from her duty but aid her in any and every way he could. She was his, if she was but willing to take a chance on him.

* * * *

Pure pleasure raced through Cherub and she muffled her cries against Kirk's neck. His cock pulsed in her hand just the same way as her inner channel pulsed around his fingers. When he'd slid his hand over her entrance and touched her very core, nothing had ever brought her such pleasure. He'd devoured her with his kisses and bites, as if he knew exactly what she needed and how to deliver it. Even now, he continued to slowly caress his fingers inside her as he gently brought them both back down.

She'd wanted this moment with him, just as desperately as he'd wanted it.

"Are you all right?" he whispered in her ear.

"Very." She cuddled into him and he wrapped his arms around her, his breaths coming slower until his beautiful golden eyes slowly slid shut and the long sweep of his eyelashes brushed his high cheeks. Long minutes passed. Quietly, she whispered his name, "Kirk?"

He didn't stir.

Well, it appeared she'd exhausted her mate. How interesting.

Smiling, she carefully straightened his clothing then hers. Goodness. She'd been so hungry for him, and although born in an era when a woman would never act so wantonly with a man, she was different. She hadn't remained in her true time for long before traveling the ages. And of late, she'd spent more time in the twenty-first century than here in the past. She was at home wherever her kin were, no matter the time or place.

With one finger, she touched her mate's lower lip. He held such a deep well of love within his heart and she could see why the fates had allowed their bond to take form. She'd adored each and every one of his kisses and even though she hadn't allowed a complete joining, in that moment when his seed had rushed forth from him and coated her fingers, she'd secretly wished his essence had instead spurted deep inside her.

More than a thousand years old and she'd never once been bedded. From the very beginning she'd chosen to remain alone, not once experiencing any desire to lie with a man. Those emotions had been a clear warning, that she would one day have a mate, that it would be just a matter of time before her soul became bound to another's. It was as Nessa had said. There was only one…for both of them.

Kirk's hold on her loosened as he fell deeper into sleep.

With a sigh, she wriggled free, her fingers so sticky. She'd wash up then wake him. Slippers kicked off and skirts scrunched high, she waded into the lapping surf and dunked her hands.

"Cherub?" Kirk groped the sand then scrambled to his feet, his wakefulness hitting him the moment she'd left his side.

"I'm right here, my tempting bear."

Eyes closed, he breathed deep and followed his nose toward her. "I can scent you."

"And what do I smell like?"

"You smell like sweet honey right now." He dropped to his knees in the water, clutched her waist and burrowed his nose into her belly. "It's completely intoxicating. I didn't mean to fall asleep. I was just so content and I've hardly gotten any rest of late. I've been too anxious as I awaited this night."

"You didnae offend me, so say no more about it." She buried her hands in his silky black locks as the surf splashed his pants and molded the black leather to his thighs. "You're getting wet."

"I care little about the water, only being close to you. My bear also wishes to meet you, actually he demands it." He rose, gripped the hem of his billowy white tunic, hauled it over his head and pitched it toward her cloak on the beach. He kicked off his boots then extended one arm. His skin rippled with fur as dark and as silky as the hair on his head, there one moment then gone the next.

"If you need to shift then do so. I'd like naught more than to see your other half, even as furry as he is."

"He might get a little possessive. He knows you're ours."

"There is naught you can do that will scare me, if that is your concern."

"I'll need to lose these pants so I can Change. Shredding my clothing is a pain in the butt and I prefer not to do it. Can you handle a little more nudity?"

"I believe I can." She licked her lips and near panted at the thought of seeing him fully unclothed. Oh dear, she was far more than just wanton. She was downright greedy. She stepped closer, stroked across his broad shoulders gleaming in the moonlight then traced one finger down the center of his wide chest and along the dusting of hair narrowing between his impressively hard abs and disappearing below the waistband of his pants. Only minutes ago she'd touched him below and doing so had brought her such pleasure. She swept her finger along his trim waist, back and forth as her desire to touch more of him flooded her once again.

Kirk caught her hand in his, his lips lifting. "My elusive imp, should you touch me again as you did just before, then I won't be held responsible for my actions. My cock is already trying to spear right through my pants for more of your exquisite attention."

"Then shift."

"As you wish." He shoved his pants down his heavily muscled legs, stepped out of them and tossed them aside. Under the moon's glow, he stood before her, so magnificently male and all hers.

Goodness, 'twas just as well he couldn't see how desperately she wanted him. Living more than a thousand years without any true companionship wasn't easy, and with him offering himself to her on a platter, the thought of leaving him was becoming more difficult by the minute. "Make the Change, Kirk." Husky words, which barely made it past her lips.

"Don't leave me while I'm in my other form." He fumbled to find her, grasped her face between his hands and brought her mouth to his for a searing kiss before he backed up and in a burst of brilliant lights, shifted and dropped to all fours. A big bear, his pelt a stunning midnight-black, lumbered toward her. He rose up on his hind legs and roared, his growl demanding all stayed far away from this place.

She swished through the lapping waves onto the sand and as she moved, he stalked her. She halted, held out one hand and he stuck his muzzle into her palm and licked her. Giggling, she knelt. "Your bear is beautiful, Kirk."

He rubbed the side of his body against her, almost knocking her over. She wrapped her arms around his neck to keep herself in place then stroked down his back and petted between his ears. When she stopped, he flopped down, rolled onto his back on the dry sand and exposed his belly.

"Do you wish for a tummy rub?"

One long rumble, which reverberated deep within his chest.

"That sounded like an aye to me." Hands spread over his belly, she stroked and as she did, he closed his eyes and fairly purred. There was naught more stunning to see than his bear. She laid down beside him and snuggled against his side. This was one of the most magical nights she'd ever had, and with her mate allowing her to see both sides of him, it made it even more special. Although what kind of a mate was she when she wouldn't even show him her true form?

"I'm sorry," she murmured in his ear. "You deserve so much more than to be bound to me, a woman who remains from your sight when you're fully prepared to show me all of you."

He growled and in a bright array of lights, swiftly made the Change then loomed over her, his dark hair falling forward over his brow as he narrowed his gaze on her chin.

"Look higher." She caught his face and directed his gaze to hers. "See, I hide from you. I'm sorry to cause you that pain."

"It's a pain I can bear, and you're only doing so in an attempt to protect me. The moment I have your image in my mind, it'll make our separation all the harder, whereas right now, I have only the knowledge you've shared. Blue eyes and blond hair. But I know exactly what counts, and that's what's on the inside and deep within your heart. You have such pure intentions and think only of others. You're all I could ever desire in a mate."

Tears misted her gaze and trickled free. She sniffed and he frowned.

"You're not crying are you?"

"Nay." She wiped the tears away but more rose and slid free.

"Damn it. You are. I can sense your lies." He traced across her cheeks and growled again when he encountered the wetness. "Please, don't cry. I never meant for my words to bring you any pain."

"They are good tears."

"No tears are good." He shoved to his feet and lifted her to hers. "What can I do to bring those giggles back?"

"Mayhap 'tis what I can do for you instead that will lighten my mood. Clothe yourself and I'll take you somewhere special." She stuck her slippers on, swung her cape over her shoulders and tied it in place.

He donned his clothes, boots and weapons, and she tried desperately not to sneak a long look at his deliciously hard body while he did.

Once he was dressed, she stepped up to him, wrapped her arms around his waist and settled her cheek on his wide chest. "I'm about to take you for a look at my world, and when I do, you'll experience a sense of weightlessness as we move through the sky. I'll also extend my cloaking to cover you. I can do so with others when needed."

"Wait." He shook his head. "I just realized. You must have been the one who opened the portal that brought me and my brothers through into this time. Isla too."

"I was. You never once thought it was me?" He'd said he'd heard the legend of the Fae Angel of Love.

"I didn't put the two together until right now. I didn't see you within the portal."

"Aye, just as you cannae see me in this moment."

"Right. The legend remains strong." He nodded. "Will this experience be similar to that trip through the portal? There was a ton of wind swirling about and a whole lot of freefalling."

"I'm sorry that occurred, but it willnae this time. When one holds onto me while traveling through a portal, there is only the enjoyment of the flight. There will be no need for a portal though right now, just a pleasant night drifting through the sky. You will soar as I will, as if on the wings of a bird."

"Well, that sounds like the kind of ride I wouldn't want to miss out on."

"Then make sure you dinnae let go of me, otherwise there will most definitely be a whole lot of freefalling involved."

"Letting go of you right now will be impossible, not now

that I've finally found you." He dipped his head, planted a kiss on her ear then groaned. "I was aiming for your mouth."

"My mouth is here." She lifted onto her toes and touched her lips to his. "Kiss me, Kirk, and we shall soar to the stars together."

"Mmm, and I only wish in more ways than one." He kissed her with a wild passion she couldn't help but respond to, and slowly, she lifted them higher and dipped and dived through the air, as in control of her element as she could be when he continually sent her thoughts awry.

Aye, the mated bond was a precious thing, and she only wished she never had to lay hers with him aside. Her mate was her match in every way, a man she could so easily fall in love with.

She bobbed over the village and drew in a deep breath. Below, smoke curled from several of the thatch-roofed houses and wisped into the night sky. Children dashed about the cottages, barefoot as they played tag, their squeals reaching her and tugging at her heart. Around a fire pit in the center of the village, both young and old chatted. Her people would always need her, just as she'd always need them. She wasn't just a time-walker but their princess. That she could never forget.

One night. She'd continue to enjoy this one night, cherish and hold it tight.

That she could do.

Chapter 2

High on the castle's battlements, Nessa stood, her plaid wrapped around her as the dawn sun peeked over the ocean's horizon. A radiant haze of red speared through the lightening blue sky and the twinkling stars above disappeared one by one until only one star remained. Eyes closed, she made a wish on it for Cherub—that the Fae Angel of Love who'd now been soul bound to another, just might find a way to make things work so she'd need never be alone again.

Aye, Cherub had said she couldn't take a mate. She'd been gifted with the greatest of their fae skills, one that required every ounce of her time and intense dedication. Bringing soul bound mates together brought her great joy and she reveled in all she did. So too would Kirk. He was a man who'd stand by his mate and aid her in whatever way he could. He would protect and care for her, ensure her safety and that her dedication to her duty never faltered. Cherub needed Kirk just as much as Kirk needed her. If only her friend would open her mind to all the possibilities, then her joy in all she did would grow even stronger and deeper.

With her inner sight focused on Cherub, she sought aid on what she needed to do to convince her friend to take a chance on her newly discovered bond. Images swirled and she grasped ahold of them, only none were of Cherub but instead their enemy, Colin MacKenzie, the Chief of MacKenzie.

Colin MacKenzie stormed the darkened lower passageways of his castle, his captain at his side. The MacKenzie clenched his fists, his shaggy brown hair plaited into war braids and knotted together with a thick strip of leather at his nape. "I willnae be defeated, and certainly no' by Gilleoin," he muttered. "I want control of the waterways between us and the Isle of Skye and for that I need his Matheson lands on the tip of Loch Alsh. I will hold dominion over that land, and by whatever means I can ensure it."

"Gilleoin protects those within the village with his very life." His captain spat the words through the gap in his buckled front teeth.

"Aye, the fae have mingled with his Matheson line and he does no' care to give up the added abilities his offspring now carry. Worse, Gilleoin and his progeny will continue to grow from strength to strength if I dinnae put a halt to it."

"What's your plan, Chief?"

"There is only one plan." He punched one fisted hand into the other. "Afore the village was to be burnt to the ground, which you failed at ensuring, I was after one woman. Find her and bring her to me. She is the answer I seek. She alone will be able to provide what I need to ensure my plan reaches completion."

"Aye, Chief. I'll go and bring her back myself." The captain strode away and Nessa's vision dissolved.

The Chief of MacKenzie wouldn't be halted in his drive to take their land. The man was a menace, one relentless and fierce menace. Except which one of the fae women from the village could he possibly be after? She needed to find out. She hurried down the stairs and into the bailey. Finding Gilleoin and imparting all she'd just learnt was imperative.

Chapter 3

With her cloaking veil extended over Kirk, Cherub bobbed through the dawn sky as the sun's rising warmth flared across the land below. A wash of golden-yellow bathed the forest's treetops and shimmered across the castle's fortified walls, while in the distance behind it, the hills rose lush and green with a wealth of new growth.

She smiled at Kirk over her shoulder as he tightened his hold around her from behind, not that he could see her or even she see him while they were both cloaked. "This land is so stunning with its lochs and bens and grassy moors. There is nowhere on Earth quite as beautiful as Scotland."

"I take it you've traveled far and wide?" His warm breath feathered across the top of her head, his question one of a hundred or more he'd asked her during the night. She'd done her best to answer those questions she could, in fact had thrived on having someone to share such a deep and meaningful conversation with. Her questions for him too had been endless, and he'd graciously shared all she'd asked of him.

"I've traveled the whole world over, many times and of course throughout the ages, but the Highlands are my home." This night with him had been magical, yet the end of it now lay in sight and even though she didn't wish for that moment to arrive, it unfortunately had. "Do you wish to collect your skiff from the village, or shall I return you to the castle instead?"

"The castle. One of the warriors at the village will return the skiff as needed. Where do you intend on going once we're back on the ground?" Another question she'd need to be evasive with.

"I intend to bathe and change, break my fast then tend to my day's work." No knowledge of where, even though she'd be within her chamber and inside the same castle walls as he would be. Certainly the temptation to blurt out the truth was strong, but then where would she be? Where would her people be? Thoughts of Amelia and her decision to forego her duty after accepting her soul bond with Olaf, swamped her. She couldn't choose such an all-consuming bond and allow her people to go uncared for. They came first and always would.

With her resolve set in place, she breezed lower as she swept toward the castle's postern gate.

"You've gone quiet all of a sudden. If you're tired and wish to rest, then allow me to join you." Husky words, and the hope in his tone shimmered through. "Or if you've a need to work, I'll join you in your duties. It matters not to me. I just wish to be wherever you are."

"I have so much to do this day, and for now, my duties will keep me here in this time until I've seen to the new matches being made. So many of the villagers were saved in the recent battle and new soul bonds have now formed across the ages."

"My place is at your side, just as yours is at mine. What will it take for me to convince you of that?" He squeezed her, the length of his warm body pressed against hers, so sweetly precious. She longed to remain right here with him, but that was a dream she couldn't harbor. "I will never leave you, Cherub." He nipped her ear, turned her around to face him then nibbled along her jaw in a slow and leisurely trail toward her lips. "Or ever give up on you."

"I cannae accept the bond as Amelia did." She brought them both down onto the forest trail just out of view of the gate where Gilleoin's warriors patrolled the battlements.

"You're not Amelia and I'm not Olaf. Choosing the bond doesn't mean you have to give up your duty. I thrive on a challenge. Aiding you in bringing soul bound mates together would become as much as my calling as it is yours."

"I'm sorry, but I cannae take the risk and possibly..." She needed to go, and before he actually managed to sway her mind. Swiftly, she became as one with the air and slipped out of his arms.

"Damn it, Cherub. I speak the truth." Swinging his arms wide, he searched for her. "Don't leave me. There isn't anything we can't overcome if we do so together."

"Thank you for an unforgettable night." Tears blurred her vision as she drifted higher. Leaving him hurt, bad. "Stay safe, Kirk."

"Come back here now." He thumped his chest, anguish slashing his face. "Your leaving, it cuts my very soul in two."

"As it does for me, but I cannae promise you anymore than I already have." The farther she moved away from him, the deeper her chest throbbed. Mated pairs should never be separated, that she knew to the depths of her heart, and here she was allowing that to happen. "Just know that I detest this, just as much as you do."

"Then don't leave me, because if you do, I will hunt you down, that I promise you." He growled under his breath. "My chase has only just begun. You're mine, the other half of my soul and I'm not giving you up."

"You must. Farewell, Kirk." She'd taken one night for herself and now she needed to forge ahead. Over the curtain wall, she streamed then through the bailey and up to her open window on the third floor. She fluttered inside, her heart a heaving mess as she materialized in her chamber. Remaining cloaked, she gripped the windowsill.

Outside, a fierce roar echoed and Kirk stormed through the postern gate into the inner courtyard. He marched toward the training warriors, on a direct course toward his brothers. Iain and Finlay were both identical to Kirk in every way, from their shoulder-length locks of midnight-black hair to their wide chests and towering height.

At the sight of Kirk's clear frustration, his brothers left the warriors and steered Kirk toward a quiet corner of the yard, right underneath her window.

"What's happened?" Iain, the eldest of the three, gripped Kirk's shoulder as he eyed him. "I got a blast of contentment along our brotherly bond last night, and I still sensed only satisfaction from you until a mere minute ago."

"I was far beyond content until my mate disappeared, right into thin air." Hands clenching and unclenching at his sides, Kirk blew out a long breath. "I found her as soon as I reached the village, although I've yet to actually see her. Cherub is the faerie king's eldest child. She's also known as the Fae Angel of Love and is one of only three time-walkers born to the fae. She can cloak herself and remain unseen, or if she wishes, move into mist form and become as one with the very air itself. So too her duty to her people is strong and she ensures those who are soul bound and separated across time, are brought together."

"I've heard of her." Iain nodded.

"As have I. Dad's spoken the tale of the Fae Angel of Love from time to time." Finlay sheathed his sword in his side scabbard, his blue tunic fluttering free over his belted plaid. Sheathed wrist daggers glinted from under his cuffs, just as they did from under Iain's.

All three of these men were warriors of great strength, although what made them the most powerful was the depth and devotion of their brotherly bond. They would do anything for each other, even lay down their life. That she'd learnt during a small number of secret visits to Kirk's home over the past few years. She'd had a need to take one of her wounded people to Dr. Tavish, their clan physician, for his highly skilled aid, which she'd been unable to procure for her clansman here in the past. Twice, in her cloaked form, she'd snuck out of Tavish's medical room to watch the brothers since Nessa had told her that one day they'd be known as the 'power of three.' Her curiosity in them had been strong, and now would always remain so because of her bond with Kirk.

"I'll need a plan of attack, and I need it now." Kirk ground one booted foot into the stony yard. "I won't lose her."

"And we won't let you lose her either. We'll help you find her." Iain crossed his arms. "What else have you got on the elusive Fae Angel of Love?"

"I'll detail all I've learnt." Kirk slid one hand into his pants pocket and removed the strand of hair he'd taken from her, his gaze softening. Around one finger, he curled it. "Amelia is another time-walker, a close friend of Cherub's. Amelia lives here at the village and is wed to a man named Olaf. They have a son named Joseph who holds the skill of foreknowledge. Amelia and Olaf are soul bound and when they joined, Amelia spoke a spell that ensured Olaf's soul became tied to hers, so for however long she lives, is however long he lives. Amelia also gave up her mantle when they joined as one, which means Cherub is the only time-walker here on Earth who can continue to do what must be done."

"Wait." Finlay frowned. "Are you saying that once you catch your mate and you join together, you'll be an immortal as she is?"

"Aye, except Cherub has no intention of joining with me. Too many of her fae kind rely on her, even more so now than ever before. Since we saved the fae village, both our clan and Murdock's have seen a new wave of unmated males sensing their chosen ones, and even though I assured her I'd never halt her in her duty, would do all I could to aid her, she's still seen what's happened to Amelia and has no intention of trekking down the same path."

"Then you'll need to keep on reassuring her, until she believes you, and we'll do whatever it takes to make certain she knows you speak the truth." A fiercely determined look crossed Finlay's face.

"Here, here," Iain decreed. "We may be the 'power of three,' but we aren't complete until we've all joined with our chosen ones." He squeezed Kirk's shoulder. "Let's train and then begin our search for her. Take comfort in the fact that since you've found her once, you can find her again. Even the Fae Angel of Love can't hide forever."

"Searching for her will be a mission since she can flitter about unseen." Kirk pocketed her strand of hair then swung his sword free, his determination once again soaring. "I'll never give her up though, not until my dying day. I just have to figure out a way to convince my mate that I speak the truth, that I'd never fail her."

"Your intentions are pure, your word always true." Finlay swung his blade in a wide figure eight. "She'll come to learn that as well. We'll make sure of it." He motioned toward the training area and the three of them strode back to the battling warriors and joined the fray.

Could she possibly have it all? Would Kirk truly aid her in her duty and not halt her in the least? His brothers had stated empathically that he would. Olaf had certainly never made such a promise to Amelia. He was a gentle man, a fisherman and not a warrior. Amelia too was a sweet and tender woman, a nurturer who longed to care for her husband and son. Amelia had been deliriously happy when the bond between her and Olaf had taken form. Olaf was her match in every way, and when she'd given up her mantle, Amelia had been more than ready to settle down in one place rather than travel through the endless streams of time.

She would never be able to settle in that way, not when she thrived on the coming hunt. Finding those who were soul bound and bringing them together across time was a thrill she'd never relinquish. A level of doubt in her decision to forego their bond rolled through her.

Kirk twirled his blade, his shoulders and arms so thick and strong and packed with muscle. Her fingers tingled with the need to touch him again, to stroke those muscles then slide her fingers through his silky black hair and tousle those gorgeous locks into complete disarray. She'd been gifted with a soul bound mate she completely adored and she couldn't halt the rush of hope that rolled through her. Mayhap she should talk to Nessa about her decision and see what she thought. A seer could see so much more than any other and she certainly trusted her friend and her wise judgment.

Below in the yard, Kirk advanced on Iain, his weapon held high. The two swung and their blades clashed, steel ringing loud against steel. Finlay jumped into the fight and the three battled, each landing one hard blow after another. They trained swiftly and without hesitation, so in tune with each other's strikes that they moved gracefully yet powerfully as one.

"My lady?" A knock sounded. "It's Effie. Are you in?"

"I'm coming." She opened the door and uncloaked her form. Only two maids ever served her when she stayed here, Effie or Maggie. Both lasses held a touch of fae blood and were loyal kin. They certainly tended to her needs and did all she asked of them. "How did you know I'd be here this morn?"

"Nessa said you arrived last eve at the village and to bring you a tray and a bath." Effie carried a tray holding a steaming bowl of oats and a trencher of sliced meats inside and set it on the side table. "She'll be up shortly."

"Wonderful. I need to speak to Nessa."

A shuffle sounded in the passageway and she cloaked

herself as two lads, not of fae blood, heaved a tub between them. Barefoot and with sooty marks on the knees of their loose-legged brown breeches, they set the tub before the fireplace. Another maid entered, set a drying cloth and bar of soap next to the tub then left with the lads.

Effie knelt at the hearth, tore strips of bark from a log and brought a flame to life striking flint with a dagger. She added a log or two and the fire soon roared and spread its heavenly heat throughout the room. The maid rose and dusted her hands against her aproned sides as she crossed to the golden curtained ambry. "What do you wish to wear this day, my lady?"

"The pale blue gown, please. Leave it on the bed if you could."

The maid removed a gown of silk, one of her favorites that matched the color of her blue eyes to perfection. Effie draped it over the black fur cover at the end of her bed then set the matching pair of slippers beside it.

The lads soon returned with pails of steaming water and Effie directed them then added vanilla scented oil and a sprinkle of dried rose petals. Done, she walked to the door and dipped her head to Nessa as she arrived.

"Thank you, Effie." Nessa closed the door behind the servants after they filed out then leaned against the door in her bronze skirts, her red locks wisped with gray coiled high upon her head. "And how is my favorite time-walker this day?"

"As well as can be considering I spent the night with Kirk." She uncloaked and hugged her friend. "What of you, Nessa? How do you fare?"

"I'm completely intrigued and dying to know all that occurred last eve. Come and eat while we talk." Nessa grasped her hand, walked to the side table, pulled out a chair for her and perched in the one opposite her as she sat. When she stayed here at the castle, they always broke their fast together, just the two of them. 'Twas a special time, one of the rare moments when she wasn't alone as her duty so often demanded.

"Well, Kirk's shifter senses led him directly to me, although I'm no' surprised." She lifted the small bowl of honey and swirled it over top of hers and Nessa's hot oats then slid a spoonful into her mouth. Delicious, and just what she needed to warm and fill her belly. "I'm sorry I first asked you to do the impossible last eve and keep him from leaving the keep."

"There wasnae a chance I could halt him. He whipped right by me, so eager to begin the chase. He's been looking for you for such a long time." Nessa patted her hand. "You must understand. The 'power of three' willnae be at their strongest until each have joined with their chosen ones, which means you must consider allowing the bond to take."

"I have to admit I now feel so torn." She bunched her hands in her lap, twisted her fingers in her skirts. "I spent the entire night in his company, even took him into the skies. I've never allowed myself such a frivolous time with another."

"He's your match in every way and all yours if you will but open your heart to him." She gestured toward the window where the sounds of steel clanging and warriors grunting echoed toward them. "Kirk will be driven to see to your needs, to aid you in all that you do. He will also never be at peace until the two of you have completed the bond and joined as one. You must accept your destiny is about to change. You need never be alone again, Cherub. Take a step of faith and accept what should be."

"I cannae deny I want him."

"Then give yourself the future you both deserve." With a heartfelt smile, Nessa stirred a teaspoon of honey into her steaming tea. "And so says the wise seer."

"Aye, very wise, but there is also pain in living an endless life as I do. Kirk is so close to his brothers and there would be desolation as Iain and Finlay aged and passed away and he did no'. That is the kind of pain I have come to accept for myself, but 'tis also the kind of pain I would never wish on another."

"Yet that should also be his choice to make and not yours." Nessa sipped her hot drink. "I've known you for a very long time, adored each and every one of the days we've been friends. I would hate to think I might have missed out on all the years that have passed between us simply because you feared the pain you'd experience when the end must inevitably come for me. I know, deep in my heart, that even when I am no longer here to watch over my people, that you will be. Iain and Finlay will feel the same way with Kirk. He will always be there for their children, grandchildren and so forth throughout the ages. 'Twill be a blessing for them to know their brother will be able to watch over their closest when they cannae."

"I never considered that."

"Aye, you'd also be giving your mate the chance to make a wonderful difference, to bring joy to those who continued to live on. His brothers will forever remain alive in their offspring's memory because he will still be here to impart his memories of them."

Nessa's heartfelt words rang deeply in her soul. She blinked away hot tears, selected a bacon slice from the trencher and chewed it. "I will consider your advice and wise words."

"Then that is all I could ask for." Nessa nodded. "Oh, we must also speak of another matter that has now arisen. I had a vision this morn surrounding the Chief of MacKenzie. It appears our enemy willnae stand down even though he lost the recent battle at the village. He still desires control of the waterways between us and Isle of Skye and covets Gilleoin's land at the tip of Loch Alsh. In my vision, he spoke of finding a woman from the village afore it was to be burnt to the ground. I've no idea who that woman is, but he's now sent his captain to find and bring her back. I've informed Gilleoin of what I've seen and he's left to increase the patrols at the village and along the coastline."

"The MacKenzie is a snake." The man would always desire more than what he owned and controlled, his thirst for domination all that drove him. "I'll keep an eye on him too, although I'll need you to remain alert for any further visions."

"Of course. I'll keep you informed should I have any." Nessa quirked a curious brow. "And in what way shall you keep an eye on Colin MacKenzie?"

"By the usual means." She'd snuck into the MacKenzie's keep from time to time to ferret out information. Caring for her kin meant ensuring their continued safety and survival and she did so by whatever means was necessary.

"You intend to visit him?"

"I will, but I'll ensure he isnae aware I'm there."

"Aye, you are impossible to detect, to capture, or to contain." Nessa stood and knelt at the tub, swirled her hand through the water. "This is the perfect heat. Come. Have your bath afore the water cools."

"I long for a hot bath." She kicked off her slippers, tossed her fur cloak over the top of the dressing screen and shed her gown before stepping into the tub. After sinking into the glorious water, she rested her head on the rim and allowed thoughts of Kirk to roll through her mind. Nessa had told her she needed to allow the bond to take. What if she did? For a moment, a true sense of peace spread through her and wonder filled her heart and made her soul sing with hope.

"Oh goodness. I truly do want him, Nessa." She leaned one elbow on the rim and looked at her friend. "So much I'm not sure I could walk away from him a second time should we meet."

"You spent the entire night with him, which means deep in your heart, you've already allowed a certain level of the bond to take. Even the Fae Angel of Love deserves to have her own chosen one. If you claim him, just as he wishes to claim you, then you need never be alone again. He is the only one you will ever be soul bound to, and you cannae allow this chance to claim your new destiny pass you by." Nessa knelt and lathered the soap. "Allow me to aid you in detangling your hair. It's been whipped into a mighty mess from your travels last eve. Dip down and wet it for me first."

"Kirk is such a temptation." She slid under the water then emerged with a sigh. "He even showed me his bear."

"His bear has been so antsy since his arrival." Nessa worked the suds through her hair then bade her to rinse the bubbles out. After she had, her friend gently detangled her locks, separated her hair into sections and ran the comb through it.

A thunderous roar reverberated from beyond the curtain wall and echoed all around.

Nessa rose and glanced outside, hands curled around the edge of the windowsill. "Kirk's gone, and likely into the forest to shift."

"I hate the thought of causing him such pain, and honestly, to have a lifetime with him at my side and aiding me in my duty, would be a dream."

"A dream you could make a reality if you so desire it." Nessa passed her a folded drying cloth from the side table. "You should speak to him again afore you make your final decision."

"What would I do without you, Nessa?" Smiling, she hopped out of the cooling water and dried herself, donned a shift then picked up the pale blue gown the maid had left and eased it over her head. The soft satin folds shimmered over her hips and swished to her ankles.

"The same could be said for me. What would I do without you? Here, allow me to lace your stays." Nessa turned her by the shoulders and cinched her gown together. "You must come and meet Isla and Arabel as well. Iain and Finlay's mates are a delight and mayhap if you see them and how happy they are, you'll see that Kirk would offer you the same level of happiness. He is a man of his word."

"Even though I brought Isla through the portal, as well as Kirk and his brothers, I did so without any of them knowing I was there. 'Tis always best that way, otherwise explaining myself leads to far too many questions when their journey isnae about me but about their quest." She slid the matching slippers on, pinched her cheeks in the looking glass and with her ability to command her element, waved the warm air from the fire through her pale locks and dried them. From the side table, she fetched her favorite silver pins embedded with diamonds and fastened one on each side and once done, nodded at Nessa. "I'm ready."

"As am I." Nessa opened the door.

She cloaked herself and followed the seer into the passageway. Even though so many within the castle held fae blood, she still preferred to come and go as much as possible without being seen.

She strolled down the winding stairs and entered the great hall devoid of almost a soul. A maid cleared the trenchers away from the trestle tables, while another maid shooed a large brown-haired dog guzzling scraps, outside.

At the dais, two young women chatted and sipped tea. Isla and Arabel. She'd never mistake either of them. A wide smile graced Isla's face, and her richly colored red gown with its white silk edging the sweetheart bodice, highlighted her flushed cheeks.

"'Tis good to see Isla and Arabel so happy." Cherub touched her heart. Isla had denied the mated bond for five long years, remaining on the run each time the full moon had arisen. As a fae-blooded shifter who held the skill to compel, Isla had managed to keep one step ahead of Iain in his fierce chase. Thankfully though, the two of them had come together and accepted their destiny. They'd completed the bond and in doing so, Isla had conceived a new merged line between hers and Iain's shifter clans. That had been the moment when the prophecy Nessa had spoken at the birth of Gilleoin's sons had flared into glorious life. The prophecy shimmered through her mind.

Gilleoin's sons will separate when they come of age and rule their own clans, yet there will come a time far in the future when a mated bond forms between the two clans. Only then must Gilleoin's descendants once again merge, and the 'power of three' be unveiled.

That unveiling had then allowed her to open a portal in the future and bring the travelers through. All was as it now should be. Iain and Isla were together, and so too Finlay had found Arabel and completed the bond. Aye, and now it was Kirk's turn, if she but allowed their bond to take.

She sighed. Nessa was most certainly right. Those who were mated were brought together for a reason and even she couldn't deny the depth of need rolling through her. Her soul rejoiced at the thought of joining with Kirk, and curled up with distaste at the thought of leaving him behind.

"Nessa!" Isla waved out as she stood, her long brown locks swaying. She nabbed Arabel's hand and hurried across the hall toward them.

"Good morn, my dears." Nessa hugged Isla then Arabel.

"Good morning to you too." Isla pressed her palm to her heart. "Arabel and I have a great need to speak to you, in private if you don't mind."

"Not at all. The chief's solar is free since Gilleoin's ridden out." Nessa motioned them into the antechamber at the side of the hall. "Whatever is this all about?"

Isla walked inside and sat in the padded chair near the unlit fireplace. "Arabel and I have a very secret mission we wish to embark on, one we need your aid in ensuring its success."

"Well, I do love a good secret mission." Nessa closed the door.

Still unseen, Cherub perched on the corner chair near the window. The room held the chief's large wooden desk, a tall chest with ornately carved feet and intricately styled doors, as well as an array of chairs and benches placed around the perimeter of the room. A fresh breeze blew in through the open window and brushed over her skin.

"This is far more than just a secret mission." Arabel crouched before the hearth, lit one fingertip with her fae fire-wielder skill and set the wood ablaze. She rose and rubbed her hands together, the white ribbon at the top of her sapphire gown fluttering. "'Tis a mission of great need as well."

"Then do tell all," Nessa urged as she glanced from Arabel to Isla.

"Arabel and I intend to wed our mates." Isla leaned forward, hands planted on the tartan draped over the arms of her chair. "But to do that we need a clergyman. There's also a catch. Iain and Finlay aren't to know what we're organizing. We wish for it to be a surprise."

"Oh, I also love surprises." Nessa grinned.

"Wonderful, because we need your aid in finding a clergyman."

"I can most definitely aid you with that." Nessa nudged the quill and ink bottle sitting on the chief's desk into the center then leaned against the edge. "The nearest priest would be Father John at the priory. I could send a guard to fetch him, and provided he was free to travel, you could be wed to your men afore the week's end."

"That sounds per—"

The door swung open and Iain strode in.

Isla raised a brow. "Well, hello, my big bear. Have you finished your training for the morning?"

"We finished early. Kirk's in need of aid, and it appears there can be no further delay." Iain crossed to her, gripped the sides of her armchair then bent and rubbed his nose against hers. "He's just changing then he'll join us. He shredded his clothes just before when he was forced to shift. His bear rides him hard and demands the return of his mate."

"I thought he found her last night. You sensed only

contentment from him."

"Aye, although she escaped him at dawn. His mate's name is Cherub and she's a fae time-walker, a woman born centuries ago to the King of the Fae." He lifted Isla from her padded chair then sat down and cradled her in his lap.

Cherub barely stifled her giggle. Those in the future were far more open with public displays of affection than those here in the past ever were, and having lived in the future, she'd adored seeing the changes in relationships that had occurred over time.

Near the far wall, Arabel gasped then slowly sighed with a silly grin on her face.

Nessa patted her heart, the sight of the two so in love clearly bringing her great pleasure too.

"I've heard the legend of the Fae Angel of Love, and of course my father's mentioned Cherub to me a time or two." Isla cuddled into Iain. "She was there when he lost my mother and she comforted and consoled him. I believe they speak when needed, but I've never actually met her and honestly, Dad's a little secretive about her and all she can do."

"Kirk said Cherub told him that there are three time-walkers. One resides beyond the veil, and the other is at the fae village."

"Aye, that is right." Arabel tucked a lock of her golden hair behind her ear. "Her name is Amelia and she is mated to Olaf, although she gave up her duty ten years ago when they wed. Amelia used to be able to control the air element, and she still can, but only to a very small degree since she's allowed her skill to wane so greatly. She and Olaf have a son named Joseph who holds the skill of foreknowledge."

"Have you met Cherub?" Iain asked her.

"Nay, she is very elusive and cloaks herself most of the time."

"Good morning, everyone." Finlay marched in, swept Arabel into his arms and plastered a kiss on her lips. She caught her breath and clutched ahold of him. "What have I missed?" he whispered against her lips. "Apart from you, my sweet."

"We've been talking about Kirk's mate."

"Kirk's desperate to find her, and we'll need to aid him in whatever way we can." Finlay nipped Arabel's ear.

Shifter men. They were always nibbling on their chosen ones, marking them however and wherever they could. Heat flushed Cherub's cheeks as she remembered marking Kirk last night and him marking her in return. She palmed her mark, right over the sensitive skin of her neck and held it closer to her.

"Sorry to be late." Kirk strode into the solar, a grim expression on his face and his black hair curling damply onto his shoulders. He must have had a quick wash and now looked completely edible in tan rawhide pants and a white tunic under a fur vest, his sword belted at his side. It certainly took all her willpower to remain right where she was and not rush into his arms. Aye, spending the night with him had allowed an element of their bond to take and denying her need for him right now tore at her.

Firmly, he closed the door, leaned against it and crossed his arms. Those wonderfully broad shoulders of his stretched ever so wide and made her fingers itch to stroke over them.

"I take it Iain and Finlay have updated you all on my elusive mate?" Kirk asked the ladies.

"They have." Nessa answered for them. She crossed to Kirk and laid one hand on his arm. "You should know that I've actually spoken to Cherub this morn and she told me of your mated bond taking form."

"You have?" He jerked upright. "I have to find her. Do you know where she went after speaking to you?"

"I can assure you Cherub is never far away." Nessa smiled softly. "You need only call to her and she will come. 'Tis her duty to aid those of fae blood, of which you hold a touch, even though none of the skills of the fae."

The breeze lifted and blew through the open window and made Cherub's hair tickle her face.

Kirk sniffed and growled then pushed off the door and prowled toward her. "I can scent my mate. It seems she's rather close indeed."

She rose to her feet.

'Twas time to make her decision, on whether she accepted the bond or not.

No more could she delay.

Chapter 4

Air swirled into the chief's solar through the open window and Kirk fisted his hands. The scent of his woman wafted toward him, an elusive fragrance as fresh as the very air itself. Breathing deep, he prowled around the room then gritted his teeth as her scent strengthened then moved.

Kirk tapped the oak tabletop as he walked behind the chief's chunky wooden desk in pursuit of his woman. "Finlay, stand at the door," he bit out. "Iain, close the window and remain in front of it. My mate is in this solar and she isn't going to leave it until we've talked."

Iain did as he bid, closed the window then planted himself in front of it while Finlay slid in front of the door.

Nessa swished to the bench along the far wall and sat. "Kirk, When Cherub and I spoke this morn, she said she couldnae deny how happy she'd been with you last eve. I assured her you would never deter her in her duty."

"I'd stand right by her side and aid her however I could." He took one step closer to Nessa and stopped. Cherub's scent lessened and he backed up swiftly. It was so strong right here in this very place by the desk. He swept his hands out and searched along the entire area. He couldn't make his mate appear unless she wished it. "What else did you speak of?"

"Your mated bond and all that it would entail."

"Cherub made her position quite clear to me, that she wouldn't accept our bond. She thanked me for the unforgettable night then told me to stay safe, which I'll never accept. I want my chosen one, and I won't rest until I have her back."

"Then consider me back." A warm rush of air brushed his cheek and ear.

"Cherub?" Her scent wrapped around him and sent his heartbeat racing. "I need you to take solid form. I can't stand not being able to touch you."

"You speak so openly around your brothers and their mates. 'Tis reassuring that you do." Softly whispered words that held a gentle playfulness to them. "Although I would like to speak to you in private, if you dinnae mind?"

"I'll never mind. Where? Name the place." Her scent drifted away and he circled the desk as he followed her. Hell, he needed to touch her, to know she was still close.

"How about my place?"

"And where would that be?"

"Upstairs. I keep a chamber here at the castle, Nessa's doing since she insists I need somewhere to call home when I'm in this time. Third floor. The first door on your left." A giggle escaped her then her scent trailed away and disappeared, any and all trace of it now gone.

"Damn it. She's left." He growled and stormed toward the door.

"She must have slipped right past me. I'm not quite sure how she did that." With a mischievous grin, Finlay opened the door. "You've got your hands full there, and don't forget to say hello from the rest of us when you catch up to her."

"Finlay, you are the worst kind of help right now." He bounded out the door and took the winding stairs two at a time until he reached the third floor. The darkened passageway remained bare of any other, each of the doors leading from it firmly shut, the only light penetrating the corridor coming through the narrow window at the far end of the passageway. Outside Cherub's paneled door, he took a deep, steadying breath, walked inside and closed the door after himself.

A warm breeze fluttered in though her open window. It ruffled the four-poster bed's golden canopy that swept down to the polished floorboards. Before the fireplace, a large oval ring-mark around the size of a tub wet the floor, while within the hearth the remains of a fire glowed. Overtop of a silk dressing screen in the corner lay a white fur cloak, his mate's cloak. He wandered toward it and stroked the soft fur. Memories surged from last night, of him carrying her through the forest, her cloak swishing softly against his legs, then of it falling away onto the sand and being exposed to his sight when he'd tugged the ties free from around her neck. "Cherub? Where are you?"

"I'm right here." Her voice whispered from behind him, a scant foot or two away and he swung around.

"Is this your chamber alone?"

"It is. Where is yours?"

"On the second floor, although I intend to move in here. I'm not asking to share a bed, just to be closer to you. I need that, and that padded chair of yours in the corner looks comfy enough." His claws sliced out, his bear still incredibly antsy and rippling right under his skin.

"That chair appears terribly uncomfortable to me." She slid one hand over his, her touch so soft, so gentle, then she tangled their fingers together and a level of calm rolled through him. "Claws away, my tempting bear."

He drew them back in, lifted her hand to his lips and kissed her palm. Slowly, he breathed in, drawing her delectably fresh scent deep inside him. "Thank you for taking solid form, except now my bear wants to roll around with you in that bed and smother you in our scent, as do I."

"Rolling around in a bed with you sounds rather thrilling." She tugged him toward the end of her bed, gripped his shoulders and pushed him down until he sat. "Although afore we considering doing so, I would like to show you something."

"Whatever you wish." She seemed so accepting and it sent both shock and fierce need racing through him. Likely his mouth gaped open. Aye, it did. He tapped it shut.

"Nessa has convinced me that I need to be more willing to allow the bond. In truth though, I doubt I would have been able to stay away from you much longer. You are the other half of my soul and that I cannae deny." She uncloaked, so swiftly his heart lost one very necessary beat. Just as well he was sitting. Her vivid blue eyes, as glorious as a summer sky, dragged him right into her very soul. And her skin, so creamy and smooth, sparkled as if capturing the sun's rays and reflecting them.

"Am I dreaming?" He blinked repeatedly.

"Nay. There are so few I uncloak in front of because my skin is rather distracting to look upon, although I wish to be my true self with you, that's if you so desire it." An uncertain look flashed in her eyes. "You dinnae need to answer me now if you wish. Think on my offer if you prefer."

"No thinking is needed. Your skin is a distraction I will completely adore." He caught her hands and tugged her in between his spread legs then cupped her hips and kept her locked in place. "I want to see you, to never have you hide yourself from me again. How come your skin sparkles? I've never met another of fae blood whose does."

"My father's was so, and his father's afore him. It denotes the eldest born in the royal line and always has."

"How many siblings do you have?"

"I am one of seven."

"It's almost impossible to look away from you. One could almost say you're spellbinding." Reveling in her nearness, he rubbed himself against her. "Are you truly willing to accept the bond?"

"I am." Two words, and the strength behind them spoke to his very heart. "My word is the truth and always has been. I must also apologize for doubting you and your own word. I shall never do so again."

"Apology accepted, and since you're the king's eldest born is there any particular protocol I need to take care of when being around you?" He stroked around to her bottom, his hands getting lost within the mountainous folds of blue silk. Gently, he squeezed her rear. "I wouldn't want to overstep any particular mark."

"I do believe you are becoming far too familiar with me, although that I shall allow and henceforth encourage."

"Thank heavens for that, because I intend to get a whole lot more familiar with you before this day is out."

"In what way?" She wriggled around and sat on his lap, her skirts puffing around her. "And be specific."

"I want the right to kiss you, anywhere and everywhere you might please." He trailed one finger along the lush swell of her breasts pushed up by her corseted bodice edged in blue satin. Licking his lips, he leaned in and kissed the mark he'd given her on her neck. Wicked pleasure at seeing the evidence of his bite on her flesh rippled through him. He played with her hair, long golden locks that swayed about her waist, the exquisite color as bright and rich as the sun beaming in the sky out the window.

"Mayhap then we should set some boundaries to begin with." She tipped a finger under his chin and lifted his gaze back to hers.

"I love boundaries. Let me start." He took her with him as he laid down on the soft fur blanket. "Wherever you go, is where I need to go. You're not to flutter away across time without taking me with you, or disappear on me again. Never again."

"Once we have joined as one, 'twould be painful for either of us to be parted for any great length of time, the same as any mated pair, although should I get called away without any warning and need to travel quickly, then you can be assured I'll return for you the first moment I can." She threaded her fingers deep into his hair and raked her nails lightly across his scalp. His bear fairly purred at her deliciously bold touch, one of absolute claiming. "What of that for a compromise?"

"Detail the moments for when you might get called away without warning." He never intended to let her go, not now she'd finally accepted their mated bond.

"Right now we are together, but should you be elsewhere, with your brothers or so, that would be one example of when 'twould be quickest for me to just leave."

"Once we join as one, we'll have a merged link of the mind, one inherent in my shifter blood. We'll be able to speak to each other at will along a pathway known only to us, mind to mind. Can that link remain in place even across the separation of time?"

"We would need to see what worked and what didnae. You are the first shifter to mate with a time-walker, so this is all rather new."

"Tell me more about your skill then. I need to understand all you can do."

She lifted one hand and the breeze fluttering through the window played over her skin. Sunshine glimmered and her skin sparkled even brighter. Such a glorious sight to behold. "I require the constant touch of my element. To be enclosed in a room without free flowing air is difficult for me."

"Then you wouldn't have appreciated it when I asked Iain to close the window."

"Nay, not one bit." She tapped his nose. "The wind speaks to me, brings me the knowledge I need of mated pairs, so when I travel through time to locate the two who are newly mated, it is along the pathway that the wind first brought their bond to me on. To carry out my duty, there must always be fresh air surrounding me, and plenty of it."

"Duly noted. I'll never enclose you fully in a room again. I'll ensure a window or door remains open." He dipped his head and nipped her lower lip. "Where do you live? And this time be specific, very specific."

"I own several parcels of land, but only one place have I ever truly called home. On the cliffs overlooking Angel Bay is a castle, a modest one I had built in the fifteen hundreds and have renovated over the centuries. That is my most constant place of residence, one I will take you to when there is an opportunity to do so." She palmed the back of his head and nipped his lower lip in return. Her breath whispered softly across his tongue, a teasing caress that made his blood roar in his ears. "I wish for you to kiss me. I've missed you since our parting."

"Considering the sparks that flew between us last night, any kissing will likely lead to us completing the bond. Are you ready for that?"

"Last eve, I should have trusted you. This morn I have seen the error of my ways, so aye, I am ready." She kissed the tip of his nose. "Are you ready to share your life with me? My duty takes me everywhere."

"Always and forever. I'll be right by your side, just as you'll be right by mine." He urged her lips apart and lost himself within her. She tasted heavenly, all pure hunger and fiery passion. Aye, he'd been waiting five long years to find her, but she'd been waiting centuries for him even though she hadn't known it. Now, he didn't intend to let another moment pass them by. He desperately desired the completion of their bond and all that it entailed, for them to be as one, to be able to speak to each other along a merged link, and to have her speak the spell to bind his soul to hers. Need rushed through him and he plunged his tongue inside her mouth and drank in her very essence. He welcomed the raw intimacy they'd share only with each other, one he would crave for the rest of his days.

"I feel hot." She pressed her breasts against his chest and nibbled toward his ear. "Very hot."

"That is because you have far too many clothes on."

"So do you." She shoved his fur vest down his arms and tossed it onto the floor then wriggled his shirt hem free from his pants. "Is your bear feeling less restless?"

"He's purring a mile a minute." He tugged his shirt over his head, tossed it to the floor and unstrapped his sword belt.

"That is better, much better." She stroked his back, her fingers playing ever so softly across his skin, her touch just as gentle as the look in her eyes had become demanding.

"I will never leave you, not now, not ever, Cherub." He lowered his head to the curve of her neck and brushed his lips over her skin, right over her rapidly beating pulse. He sucked, hard, and she gasped and stretched her neck for more.

"Please, bite me again."

"I intend to, but only after I've adored the rest of you first." Slowly, he trailed his lips down her neck and along the low-cut neckline of her gown. Her nipples beaded and poked the pale blue silk. Cupping her breasts through the cloth, he thumbed the rising peaks. She was so responsive, every inch of her his to treasure. "My woman, my mate. I intend to kiss you, to leave not even one inch of your body untouched, then I intend to make you mine."

"Aye, please. I've waited over a thousand years for you. I almost cannae believe this moment is real, or that I might have allowed our bond to never be." She palmed his face, brought his mouth back to hers and kissed him, until the taste of her swarmed his senses and he desired a whole lot more. He licked her tongue, the inside of her mouth and heat flared through him, from his fingertips to his toes. Keeping his passion in check with her right now would be a losing battle and it was just as well he didn't have to. She'd agreed to their joining, desired it as much as he did.

More. He needed more. To feel her skin against his, her body wrapped around him, all skin on skin and nothing else. He tugged her bodice down, dipped his head and grazed his teeth over one nipple. Her full, warm breast taunted him to take more and he sucked the delectable bud deep inside his mouth and tickled the tip with his tongue.

"Oooh, that feels—oh, wait." She moaned, her fingers digging into his shoulders as she latched on and shook him. "Amelia calls. The wind ripples with her need."

"The wind what?" Desire hazed his mind.

"I must go." She disappeared and he fell onto his face into the fur bedcovers.

"Cherub?" He shoved up and searched the room. She was gone, her scent barely lingering in the air. Well, that was fiercely frustrating. His bear rumbled his displeasure at the loss of his woman and his soul cried out for her return. This couldn't happen again.

* * * *

Cherub fixed her bodice as she shimmered through the air toward the village. Amelia had called out to her, displacing the very air itself in her desperate need to make contact. That need had penetrated the fog in her head, just.

The moment she'd whisked in over the village, she breezed down and slid underneath Amelia's door, took her true form and uncloaked. "Amelia? 'Tis Cherub. I'm here."

"Thank goodness." Amelia hurried toward her from a side room, hands clasped in her deep green skirts. "I wasnae sure if you'd hear my summons considering your mate's recent arrival."

"You knew Kirk was here?"

"I was in the forest picking berries for a blackberry pie when I sensed the ripple in the air that signified your match had been made. It has been years since my skill has ever arisen in that way, but the thread linking your soul to his was so strong it near knocked me right off my feet." She hustled toward the trunk sitting under the narrow window overlooking the central village fire pit where two ample-chested women stood in aproned skirts tending to two large fire-blackened pots. "I cannae believe you're mated to a shifter, but so happy I am that you are."

"Our bond took me quite by surprise, particularly since he first sensed me five years ago and I never did." She squeezed her friend's arm. "Your call was urgent. Tell me what you need."

"Aye, I worry over Joseph." She picked up a pair of lad's breeches where they sat atop the chest and handed them to her. "He should have returned from collecting herbs near the burn more than two hours ago. Olaf has searched and cannae find him, and 'tis so unlike my son to wander off without a trace. I cannae help but worry since the MacKenzie's recent attack was such a short time ago. Gilleoin has additional patrols in this area, and we've heard of Nessa's vision, but I needed to ask you if your bear would be able to track him for me? Gilleoin and Kenneth both rode through here an hour ago toward the tip of the loch and willnae be back for some time, otherwise I'd ask them to shift and search for him."

"Of course. I'll ask Kirk to search for Joseph. We'll do so immediately." She clasped Joseph's breeches to her chest. "Where did you see Joseph last?"

"He entered the forest a little farther along the cliff-top trail. I watched him from the shoreline while speaking to one of the other village lasses. Where the rock sits beside the tallest pine tree. That is the place where you need to begin. From there, head toward the burn deep in the forest." Amelia clutched a hand to her heart, her short brown locks bobbing on her shoulders. "I have a terrible feeling that willnae leave me. 'Tis as if he is now far away. I should never have allowed my skill to decline so greatly. I can take on mist form, but only for a few seconds at a time."

"I'll find him and bring him home. Dinnae fear." Her heart ached for her friend and her declining skill. Taking on mist form was essential for a time-walker if they wished to hold onto its restorative healing power. Immortal they were, but they could still suffer an injury and only their ability to move into mist allowed for that full healing. "You must strengthen your ability and I'll aid you, until you can hold your mist form as you used to."

"Aye, and I will gladly accept your aid, but first, find Joseph for me." Tears pooled in Amelia's soulful brown eyes. "Be careful as you travel."

"I shall." She hugged Amelia, melted away and sped back to the castle. Through her open window, she slipped through then shimmered into form before Kirk. "I'm so sorry to have left you as abruptly as I did."

"It's all right. I understand." Kirk tugged his tunic over his head, his sword once again belted at his side. His golden gaze moved over her, as if he reassured himself she was well. "What's happened?"

"Amelia asked her son, Joseph, to collect some herbs in the forest near the burn and he has no' returned. Gilleoin and Kenneth have ridden to the watch-point and so she called out to me for aid. Joseph is only nine. Could you track him for her with your shifter senses? We need to find him and bring him home."

"Of course." He eyed the breeches in her hands. "I take it those are his?"

"Aye, and we are about to travel, with all speed toward the cliff-top trail where he entered the forest. I'll extend my cloaking to cover you." She seized his hand, cloaked them both and whisked them through the open window, a tight fit for two in full cloaked form but she still managed it.

A minute later, she landed along the cliff-top trail and uncloaked them.

"Whoa." Kirk swayed then found his feet. "That was incredibly fast."

"There was no time for delay. Undress, as quickly as you

can." The wind rushed up the cliff and whisked over them, bringing with it the salty scent of the sea.

"Woman," he grumbled as he set his sword belt and tunic on the top of a craggy stone next to a towering pine then removed his boots. "I hope you realize I'm now undressing for entirely the wrong reason."

"Aye, but you have my most heartfelt thanks for doing so. I promise to make this all up to you, just as soon as I can."

"Your people come first, that I understand, although I'll be counting down the minutes until you can in fact make things up to me. That's one promise I won't let you relinquish." He loosened the ties of his tan pants, grasped his waistband and shoved the leather to the forest floor.

Oh, how she wished that moment was right now. All man and hungry bear, he shifted in a sizzling display of crackling energy and searing light. His big bear prowled toward her and she stepped back and knocked her back against a wide trunk.

He rose up onto his hind legs, slapped his paws down on the rough bark either side of her head then ever so gently, rubbed his furry cheek against hers.

"Here are Joseph's breeches." She pressed them into his muzzle and he lugged in a deep breath. "Find him, my mate, and I'll forever be in your debt."

A rumble escaped his throat then he dropped down onto all fours and lumbered into the forest. Sniffing, he tracked Joseph's scent.

She scooped up his belongings and followed him along the leaf-strewn trail edged with low brush. She jumped trailing tree roots while overhead, birds twittered from high in the dense canopy and all around, small creatures scurried through the undergrowth at the presence of a predator in their midst. Kirk padded toward the burn, just as Joseph would have and going by the heavy mark of tracks along the busy pathway, so too had many others.

Suddenly, he halted then veered off the trail. He weaved in and around scraggly bushes until they left the thickness of the forest behind and a half hour later emerged before a large clearing dotted with tiny yellow flowers and lavender bushes. This area was so very far from the burn. Kirk plodded in a slow circle, buried his muzzle in the ground then shifted. On his knees in a flattened area of grass and dirt, he carefully separated the trampled stalks and plucked a small swatch of plaid from within free. 'Twas MacKenzie plaid.

She crouched next to him and tried heartily to keep her curious gaze on his find and not his gloriously naked body. Seeing him shift in the dark of night wasn't one bit the same as watching him do so under the midday sun's brilliant blaze.

"Joseph's scent is all over this strip of tartan." He traced a small, muddy footprint in the dirt. "It looks as if he's stomped it into the ground with his bare foot."

"He detests the MacKenzies, just as we all do."

"For good reason, although for this MacKenzie plaid to be here, so too a MacKenzie must have as well. I'll keep following Joseph's scent and see where it leads." He passed her the tartan. "Don't lose that, and try not to handle it too much."

"I'll keep it safe." She pocketed it and stood.

He rose and towered over her, bringing her nose smack up against his hard chest as he did.

"I—ah—" Oh goodness. He was far too close and the breeze swirled with his deliciously warm and spicy scent.

"All will be well. We'll find him." Gently, he pressed a kiss to the top of her head, stepped back and shifted. Black silky fur sprouted where there had been beautiful golden skin and his bear lumbered around her, brushed against her legs and nose to the ground, he continued across the meadow to the far side where the forest once again rose high.

She followed then halted as he did at the tree line. Several fresh track marks, both from horse and man, marred the ground and the sooty remains of a recently doused fire sat within a roughly-made stone fire pit. Kirk stuffed his muzzle into Joseph's breeches which she still held then trod around the area in ever-widening circles. He halted, let out a fierce roar that sent her pulse skittering right out of alignment before he shifted in a burst of brilliant light.

Fury darkened his face as he strode toward her. "This is the place where Joseph's scent disappears, and at a good guess, I'd say whoever was here on horseback took him with them. MacKenzies have made camp on Matheson land and damn well gotten away with it."

"What do we do?"

"They've left, not heading toward the village but back the way they've come." He pointed toward the MacKenzie's lair that lay some distance across rugged terrain and the inner channel of the loch to the northeast. "They've gotten what they wanted."

"Nessa saw in a vision that the MacKenzie was after a woman from the fae village, not a lad." She bunched her arms tighter around his clothing and weapons in hand.

"You told me Joseph holds the skill of foreknowledge. He's aware of events before they occur, correct?"

"Aye, but he would've told Amelia or Olaf of the trespassers had he seen them in a vision. He's so young, wouldnae have gone off on his own without leaving word with someone."

"Yet he clearly veered off the trail and came directly here. He had to have seen something to make him suddenly change course. Although why the MacKenzie warriors would grab him instead of the woman they're after is a mystery." He laid his hands on her arms, stroked slowly up and down. "Would Joseph have told them what particular skill he held?"

"He may have if he wished to protect his village kin. His protective urges are strong for one so young, and his is a sought after skill." Anxiously, she stepped back and paced the grass as a hawk swept the air currents high above. "Although no matter why he was taken, the MacKenzies have him and I need to get him back."

"Not just *I*"—he held out his hands for his clothes and weapons—"but *we*. *We* need to find him and return him to his parents. You're not alone anymore, Cherub. You have me, and my brothers as well if you wish. There isn't anything any of us wouldn't do to aid you."

"I'm sorry. I misspoke." She passed his clothing to him, reached up on her toes and kissed his chin. "*We* it is. Thank you, my tempting bear."

"You're the tempting one." He juggled his belongings into one arm and with his free hand, wrapped it around her waist and drew her closer. Smiling, he rubbed his body against hers, his delicious scent encasing her. "I hope you don't mind. The need to ensure you hold my scent is strong."

"I dinnae mind in the least." She slid her fingers into his silky hair, his armful of clothes and weapons now squished between them. With her palm firm around the back of his head, she brought his mouth to hers. She kissed him then whispered against his lips, "Be careful and dinnae allow that sword to slice off anything I might find useful later on."

"Never, and you are such a tease." He chuckled and kissed her back, his laughter reaching right inside her heart. Soon, they'd complete the bond and naught would ever keep them apart again, not even her earlier resolve to forego all that should be. How she'd even believed that might be possible dumbfounded her. She, the Fae Angel of Love, should have known better.

"I cannae wait," she murmured as his arousal poked her in the belly, "to join with you in all ways. Thank you for being my mate, and for dealing with my earlier uncertainties as well."

"Certain parts of me can barely wait either, and no more apologies are needed. Now, we need only focus on finding

Joseph and nothing more." He pinched her bottom then stepped back and pulled on his tunic. "Can you collect my brothers and bring them here as quickly as you can? Since there appear to be a number of warriors in this party, I'll need all the help I can get."

"Aye, I'll bring them back."

"I'll run a wider perimeter search while you're gone."

"I willnae be long." She became as one with the air, swept around him then brushed one last lingering kiss across his lips before she flew high on the breeze toward the castle.

Chapter 5

Inside her chamber on the second floor of the keep, Isla Matheson toppled back onto the blanketed bedcovers with a soft sigh, her rich red skirts settling around her as Iain bolted the door and prowled across the room toward her. She grinned at him. "You look like a hungry bear who hasn't been satisfied in a while."

"Last night feels like a lifetime ago, and rising at the crack of dawn to train with Finlay in the hope Kirk would soon return was sheer agony, particularly when I knew you lay naked in our bed." He set one knee beside her leg then sank down on top of her. "Tell me if I'm too heavy for you. I wouldn't want to squish our cubs."

"They are too little to squish, and you always feel sublime on top of me." She slid her hand over his heavily beating heart and he lifted up a touch and caressed the slight rise of her belly, one barely discernable but still there all the same. Pure joy lit his eyes, just as it had when she'd told him about Nessa's vision. The seer had seen they would have two sons, both seers. "I can't believe Kirk is mated to a time-walker. How intriguing is that?"

"Very. As lads, the tale of the Fae Angel of Love used to enthrall us. To think she's real, not just a legend at all, is incredible."

"I hope she feels comfortable soon in showing us all her true form. I'm going to love having a new sister, right alongside Arabel."

"Right now, I'd rather you feel comfortable showing me your true form." He traced one finger along the white silk edging her red sweetheart bodice. "Your breasts are fuller. Are they more sensitive?"

"They are when you touch me like that." She loosened the laces at the front of his shirt and tugged his collar to the side. The mark she'd placed on his neck three days ago had faded and the need to bite him again, to imprint her mark on him and ensure everyone knew he was hers, thrummed strongly through her. He was her mate and everything within her longed for more. "Come closer," she breathed.

"You wish to bite me?" He stretched and angled his neck for her.

"Aye, as well as to nibble on the rest of you."

"My love, there is nothing I love more than being nibbled on by you. I also love it when you get all hot and bothered and completely demanding."

"I seem to be far more demanding than usual. My bear has an insatiable appetite since I'm unable to shift while expecting." Unable to wait another moment, she razzed her teeth over his most sensitive spot then bit down and claimed the man who was hers in every way. He jerked, his breath catching then he pressed his lips to her tender skin and bit her in return. Tingles rippled through her body and she rocked against him, his bite only the beginning of all she needed.

Aye, he was hers, her soul at ease only when they came together as one.

Chapter 6

Giggling, Arabel grasped her sapphire skirts and dashed upstairs to the third floor as Finlay chased her, the one thought on his mind clear for her to read along their merged link. "'Tis the middle of the day, Finlay. What will everyone think if we disappear for hours on end?"

"I care little about what time of the day it is, only that I have you in my arms. Got you." He scooped her up then strode down the passageway to the last door and entered their chamber. With his hip, he knocked the door shut then whispered in her ear, "You are in so much trouble for running in the wrong direction. You should have been racing toward the cavern, not this room."

"I adore our cavern." The underground cave they'd claimed as theirs held a large pool of cool water and was hidden deep within the earth at the base of the cliffs farther along the loch. The cove was a place few tread to with it being beyond the marshy swampland. The cavern though had become their sanctuary and saving grace, the one place where they could safely come together as one since her fire skill reared during moments of intense intimacy.

"For now, I'll just have to steal a few kisses and a couple of bites to tide me through until we can get to where we need to be." He set her down next to the side table and poured water from the jug into the basin. "For you, just in case."

"It sounds like you intend to steal far more than a few kisses and bites." She dunked her hands into the chilly water since 'twas impossible to say no to her mate.

"Keep your hands dunked"—he brushed in behind her, swept her long blond hair to the side and exposed the column of her neck—"because I'm famished for a taste of you."

"If I burn this castle down, then 'twill be all your fault."

"Is that so?" His warm breath feathered across her skin and sent tingles racing through her body. Her nipples hardened and poked her satin bodice, a terribly delicious sensation that had her arching her back and pressing against him for more. "You want me to touch you, my sweet?"

"Aye, wherever and however you please."

"Like this?" He smoothed over her hips from behind then cupped her breasts through her gown. With his thumbs, he flicked her hardened nipples as he sucked on her neck. A deep burning need for more sent a rush of heat to her core and cascaded over and sent steam curling into the air from the basin of water. "Are you ready for more?"

"Only one bite." A desperate desire for far more raced through her. "Then we leave for the cavern."

"Mmm, very good. You are a woman after my own heart." He slid his hand inside her bodice just as he bit down and marked her. All of her throbbed, her control teetering on the edge as a wave of heat shimmered from her and rustled the bed canopy behind them. "Time to go," he murmured and crossed to the door. "Ladies first."

"One moment. I need a full dunking afore we leave." She tipped the entire basin on her head and steam plumed. That should be enough to cool her until they reached their sanctuary. She righted her bodice and brushed her sides as she walked to the door, her gown drying from one step to the next with merely a thought from her mind alone.

Finlay opened the door then frowned as Iain stood with Isla on the other side, his brother's hand raised, ready to knock. "This is really bad timing, Iain."

"I know the feeling." He motioned behind him toward nothing but the passageway wall. "Cherub is here. She knocked on our chamber door a few minutes ago. She needs our aid. A lad from the village is missing, taken by MacKenzie's men. Joseph, Amelia's son. He holds the skill of foreknowledge, a rather sought after skill. Kirk awaits us in the forest where the boy was taken. Grab your weapons. We may encounter a battle to get him back."

Chapter 7

Cherub extended her cloaking to cover both Iain and Finlay as she whisked them over the woods toward the meadow where she'd left Kirk. Collecting them had made for an interesting moment. The men had been both frustrated and yet glad to offer her aid, Iain reassuring her that whenever she needed them, they'd come, and without a moment's hesitation. With both men heavily armed and Iain carrying a war coat for Kirk, she set them all down gently in the meadow currently bereft of her mate. She uncloaked and dipped her head toward them. "Thank you both for answering my call of need."

"Whoa, how incredible." Iain's gaze widened on her. "Your skin glimmers. Has Kirk seen you like this?"

"Aye, he has. Such a glimmer is a physical attribute held only by the eldest child born within the ancient royal line. As such, since I've never had children, I'm the last to hold it."

"It must be a little difficult for you to go around unnoticed on Earth. No wonder you cloak so often." Finlay stepped forward, hugged her and smiled. "Welcome to the family, to both you and your sparkly skin. I'm going to enjoy having another sister."

"Thank you." She smiled and searched the meadow

surrounded by tall pine trees for her mate. "Kirk intended to scout around."

"Then he won't be far." Walking toward the forest trail, Iain raised his nose to the air and she and Finlay followed as he tracked his brother.

They tramped through the trees a good furlong or two before they found Kirk crouched next to a trickling stream.

"Kirk, I've brought your brothers," she called out to him.

"Perfect timing." Kirk rose and crossed to them, his white tunic flapping free under his fur vest. "The MacKenzies are definitely headed back the way they've come, toward their own land and we're after a group of five, maybe six warriors."

"Then we'll need to head them off at the pass, before they have the chance to make it back to their lair." Iain tossed Kirk a black war coat studded with bits of steel, the same as what he too had donned over his brown leather pants. "Cherub explained Nessa's vision to us, that the MacKenzie was after a woman from the fae village. The fact that they've taken a lad instead is very interesting, although Joseph does hold the skill of foreknowledge, an ability the MacKenzie would likely covet as well."

"Gilleoin will be furious when he learns Joseph was taken. We sent Arabel and Isla to update Nessa and ensure one of his guards rode out with the news." Finlay adjusted the bow and satchel of arrows he'd slung across one shoulder, his black cotun a thick jacketed padding underneath. "Children shouldn't be brought into a war. It's despicable."

"I agree, which means we need to retrieve the lad and return him to Amelia and Olaf, immediately." Kirk donned his war coat, his golden gaze sweeping over her. "We need to catch up to them as quick as we can. Can you extend your cloaking to cover us all?"

"I can extend my cloaking to shield all who are connected to me. It takes a little more concentration, although naught I cannae handle."

"Are you certain?" He slid one hand over her hip, the other around the back of her head as he brought her closer to him. "I don't want you getting hurt."

"I'm an immortal. No harm can befall me, no matter if I'm right in the middle of a melee." Goodness, the first moment she could, she would complete the bond and ensure he too was an immortal. "You're the one who needs to take care until I can speak the spell to bind a piece of your soul to mine."

"You can't do so right now?" He raised a questioning brow.

"I wish I could, but 'tis only possible in the moment when we join as one."

"I see." He dipped his head and kissed her, his lips whisper soft against hers. "I wish that were now, but it'll have to wait."

Waiting would be sheer torture. With a soft sigh, she turned in his hold so he stood at her back then extended her arms for Iain and Finlay. "No one is to let go of me during our travel through the sky, or if you do then you shall fall to the Earth, and rather fast."

"We'll keep ahold, just as we did on the trip here." Iain grasped her right arm while Finlay took hold of her left.

From behind her, Kirk nuzzled her neck, his breath a warm flutter across her skin. She wriggled her bottom into his groin and winked over her shoulder at him. "Are you ready, my tempting bear?"

"As ready as I'll ever be." He nipped her ear. "To the skies, my elusive imp."

"We'll follow the enemy's tracks where possible, although there is only one way to get to the MacKenzie's keep from here." She cloaked them all, took them into the skies, just above the trees so they could follow the main forest path.

"How fast can you move through the air?" Finlay asked from her left, as invisible as she was.

"When I am in mist form, a journey of several miles can be

done in mere moments, but transporting others as I am now is far slower since I must take into account your need to survive." She gained a little more height as the craggy hills of the Highlands rose up ahead.

"Surviving is good." Finlay chuckled. "Arabel will certainly be furious with you should you drop me, and by the way, you don't want to see her get angry. Fire shoots from her fingertips and she lights up like a storm."

"Ignore Finlay. I'll never allow anyone to harm you." Kirk's hold around her waist tightened, his chest at her back so deliciously warm. "You're mine to protect, always mine."

"As I'll never allow another soul to harm you either." A promise she would forever keep. She'd been gifted with a mate and now she'd chosen to accept their bond, she wasn't letting him go. She crossed the hills then flew down toward the other side where rolling fields of heather awash with wildflowers spread into the distance. A fast-moving river weaved through the lush green pasture, the waters streaming over wide boulders and flowing toward the inner channel of the loch only a few miles away.

"This is the most beautiful, untouched land," Kirk whispered in her ear. "I love traveling with you this way. We have a bird's eye view of it all."

"Aye, 'tis a blessing to be able to hold my skill, even though an all-consuming one." She left the fields behind as they gave way to the forest bordering the loch. She skimmed the treetops while up ahead, nestled amongst the towering pine and elm trees, a quaint stone inn with smoke puffing from its chimney, beckoned travelers.

"Divert past the inn and take us down onto the beach, right there." Kirk's fingers brushed her cheek as he directed her gaze toward a galley with the MacKenzie flag flapping from its center mast. The vessel sat half beached on the sandy shore bereft of even one soul.

"I see it. This appears to be a safe place to set us all down." She swept down and landed on the grassy verge. Across the other side of the loch lying under a pall of gray cloud, the imposing fortress of the MacKenzie keep sat with its four-story gray tower house rising tall and strong above the massive fortified curtain walls. Built on an island a stone's throw from the mainland meant one couldn't easily sneak into their stronghold. In fact, 'twas damn near impossible.

"Uncloak us all," Kirk said. "We need to find our enemy, and as quick as we can."

"Mayhap they're resting at the inn." They certainly hadn't seen them thus far. She uncloaked and swayed as black dots danced before her eyes. She blinked and righted herself.

"Are you all right?" Kirk turned her in his arms.

"Aye, I just need a moment or two to recover."

"Are you sure?" He searched her gaze.

"Very sure. I'm truly fine."

"If all's well"—Iain tipped his head toward the trail leading back toward the inn—"then let's lay low and take a wander and see where everyone else is."

"We'll be right behind you." Kirk gripped her hand. "Cloak yourself, but only you. Obviously shielding us all sapped some of your strength."

"I dinnae usually transport so many so far either." She cloaked herself as he'd asked.

"That's better." Fingers tightening around hers, he nodded.

Together, they snuck after Iain and Finlay as they crept through the thick underbrush running alongside the main pathway to the inn. A hundred yards in, they all stopped and lowered to a crouch, the underbrush keeping their position well hidden. She tucked herself in behind Kirk and rested one hand on his back so he'd know where she was.

At the side of the inn near the stables, a lad with a brown woolen cap, his dusty tunic's sleeves rolled to his elbows, brushed down a black war horse tethered to a long rail next to a corral holding several more horses. Within the wooden beamed enclosure, another lad fed handfuls of oats to the animals within.

A stout warrior wearing the MacKenzie plaid belted at his waist and a massive claymore holstered across his back, stepped out of the inn with its low hung eaves and stony facade. With a slosh of the ale within an earthenware tankard he held, he plunked it down on the front step then crunched across the stony courtyard toward the lads. Wiping spittle from his mouth, he narrowed his gaze on them and grit out, "We were never here, nor the lad we have with us. Am I understood?"

"Aye, sir. We've seen no one." The boy rubbing down the war horse dipped his head in obedience while the other lad in the enclosure nodded as he picked up a pail of water and hauled it from one horse to the next.

"Good, ensure that remains so." The warrior turned and marched toward the trail next to their hidden spot. He strode past them, within fifteen feet before disappearing through the thick line of pine trees toward the bay.

Iain motioned his brothers closer and they tightened their huddle. "We're not letting the MacKenzies take Joseph past this point. If we do, it'll be near impossible to get him back without an army in tow."

"Agreed," both Finlay and Kirk murmured.

"We stay close, cover each other's backs, just as we always have and always will. Kirk"—Iain clasped Kirk's forearm—"go and subdue the idiot that just headed toward the beach, as quickly and quietly as you can. That'll be one less man we need to worry about when the rest leave the inn. Whistle out if you need a hand. We'll remain here and alert for the others."

"Sure will, although don't forget to whistle out if you need a hand." Kirk glanced up into the dense foliage of the closest tree, swept her into his arms and hoisted her into the safety of the wide bow, her position hidden even though she was cloaked. "Stay right there where I know you'll be safe."

"I shall, provided you remain safe as well." Although naught would stop her from joining the battle if she was needed. He and his brothers were kin, and she always protected her people, no matter who the adversary. "Be careful."

"Always." He blew her a kiss then stole through the trees toward the enemy.

* * * *

High above in the canopy, birds chirped, and on the gentle sea breeze sweeping in off the water came the promise of all Kirk fought for—freedom for his clansmen. No one would take one of his or Cherub's kin and get away with it.

Stealthily, he snuck behind a wide trunk and searched the bay. The MacKenzie warrior untied the galley's rope from around a large boulder, coiled and tossed the rope inside the hull then gripped the bow and shoved the galley off the beach and into the water.

The MacKenzies were preparing to leave, and he didn't doubt the rest of the warriors would soon be heading down that trail. Leaving his brothers to battle the remainder of their enemy on their own wasn't something he'd ever do. They fought together, always at each other's sides, and now wouldn't be the exception.

He nabbed a decent sized rock, one that fit snugly in his hand then jogged as soundlessly as he could from the tree line down the beach toward the beefy warrior. The urge to teach his adversary a lesson, to never bring an innocent child into the middle of a war, thrummed strongly through him. The MacKenzies were a thorn in their sides, a constant threat against his Matheson kin, a threat he needed to send winging back home with their tails between their legs.

Boring down on the MacKenzie, he yelled, "I see you're

ready to leave."

The MacKenzie swung around, the surprise in his eyes there one moment but gone in the next. He heaved his claymore free and Kirk slung the rock at him. It hit the warrior square in the forehead and he groaned, eyes going dazed as he fell to his knees. Flinging water, he stumbled to push back up.

"No. You're going down and staying down. We honestly don't have time for a fight right now, not when I'm needed elsewhere." He whipped his sword free and slammed the hilt down on the MacKenzie's head.

The warrior slumped head first into the waves.

"Damn it." Sheesh, he didn't have time for a drowning either. He clutched the warrior by the back of his cotun, hauled him up onto the beach and dumped him on the sand. "You can thank me for saving your butt later."

A pretty trill sounded. Iain's warning.

With his sword in hand, Kirk dashed back into the trees.

A fierce battle cry rang out and he picked up his pace.

The hefty sound of steel clashing reverberated through the forest. Ahead on the trail, his brothers stood back to back with four MacKenzies battling them. Not the best of odds, or odds he'd allow to remain in place.

He bounded into the fray and whipped his blade into one of the warrior's sides.

Grunting, the warrior fell back a step. He grasped his side and eyed the long slice in his steel-studded war coat, a cut that hadn't quite drawn blood. Snarling, he eyed Kirk. "You, I will gladly kill."

"Death isn't on my agenda for the day, but a good fight is." He thrust his sword high and blocked the MacKenzie's swift blow. "Where's Joseph?" he called to Iain.

"I tossed him into a tree." Iain slammed his blade down on the MacKenzie he fought, metal clanging. "Glad you could join us."

"You don't get to have all of the fun, all of the time." He ducked his opponent's next blow then kicked the man's leg out from under him. He went down and knocked his head on a protruding rock. Skin split and blood gushed. Ouch. That had to have hurt.

He checked the warrior's breathing then assured he lived, tore a strip from his bottom of the man's plaid, wrapped it around his head and knotted it to help stem the blood flow.

"Kirk!" Finlay caught his adversary's blow then bounded out of reach of the second's swipe. "Would you cease saving the enemy and come over here and help me."

"On my way." Battling, he thrived on, but taking a man's life, he didn't. If there was no need to kill, he didn't. With his sword in hand, he jumped the low brush and came in beside Finlay. "What's taking you so long in bringing these two down?"

"They're incredibly persistent, and keep your eyes on the fight." Finlay twirled his blade as he advanced on the warrior closest to him.

The MacKenzie snarled at Finlay. "I'm no' leaving here without the boy, so you'd best get out of my way."

"He's an innocent child, and you're not taking him anywhere." Finlay met the MacKenzie's fierce strike and they battled, hard and fast.

With both his brothers at his back, Kirk fought. Sweat poured from his body while high in the canopy above, Cherub's presence and the need to get her and Joseph back to safety, rode him hard. This fight needed to end, now.

The warrior he battled swung and Kirk rocked back on his heels, barely missing the man's deadly strike. They were a blood-thirsty lot, their intention to fight to the death clear to see.

"Kirk!" Cherub cried out his name then shimmered into sight behind the warrior and swung a tree limb at him. It grazed the man's side and he snapped around and bounded toward her, his blade whizzing through the air as she disappeared in a blink.

Battle lust roared through Kirk and he attacked. No one would harm his woman and get away with it. He struck the warrior with one deadly blow after another until he swayed backward then with one swift shove, Kirk sent the MacKenzie toppling into a massive thorny bush.

The warrior yelped, tried to roll free but only sank deeper into the barbed scrub.

Cherub reappeared and dropped a rock on the man's head. He slumped, arms limp and his sword sliding free from his drooping fingers. She rushed into his arms, her hands sweeping over him. "Are you hurt anywhere?"

"No, and you were supposed to stay put in that tree." Within the bow of the closest one, a wide-eyed boy with dirt-smeared cheeks and rumpled brown hair, shivered. "You must be Joseph. Are you hurt at all?"

"Nay, sir." The lad clutched ahold of the trunk.

"Prepare to die!" The MacKenzie fighting Iain lunged at him and Iain struck, pushed him back into the trunk and speared the man's arm to the tree.

Finlay knocked his opponent onto his knees, their two blades crashing a mere breath from the MacKenzie's nose. "Concede to your defeat," Finlay barked as he loomed over the man. "Or die if you don't."

"Who are ye?" The MacKenzie heaved in a deep breath, his arms shaking as he tried to keep Finlay's blade from slicing into him.

"We're the 'power of three.'" Finlay shoved his blade down harder, right against the warrior's throat. "And I want you to return to your chief and ensure he knows we stand by Gilleoin's side. We'll never allow you to harm one of our kin, or trespass on our land again. Do you hear me?"

"Aye. I concede." The warrior slowly lowered his blade then dropped it.

"A wise decision." Finlay kicked the weapon into the brush.

"Now take your wounded and leave. With all haste."

Iain hauled his blade free of the warrior he'd impaled and the man seized his bleeding arm and stumbled to keep on his feet. "Grab those two and be gone with you," Iain snapped.

The two warriors heaved their downed men over their shoulders and lurched down the trail toward the bay. Iain followed them, his sword pressed to the back of the one at the rear.

* * * *

With the battle over, Cherub ran her hands over Kirk's body once more. No nicks or cuts. He was clear, had told her the truth that he hadn't been harmed. Needing a moment to calm herself, she clung to him.

When he'd left her sight to deal with the warrior on the beach, she'd been unable to remain in the tree and had instead breezed after him. At the bay, he'd struck the MacKenzie with a perfect stone's throw then a blow to the head that had knocked the warrior out. Although instead of leaving his enemy to drown, he'd hauled him from the surf and saved his life. So too, none of his brothers had killed the men they'd fought against. They'd unarmed them as quickly and efficiently as they could. They honored a man's life, no matter who he was, as did she. "I cannae lose you, no' ever." She buried her nose in the V at the top of Kirk's war coat and dragged in his deliciously spicy scent, one that had become essential to her senses.

"I'm not going anywhere, other than wherever you go." Gently, he stroked the back of her head, each soft caress tugging at her heart and opening it ever wider to draw him inside. Her very soul rejoiced at being this close to him, of having him all to herself, and she desperately wished to tell him of her growing feelings only this wasn't the right place or time.

Iain returned and nodded. "They've left, all of them."

Slowly, she pulled away then knelt next to Finlay as he checked Joseph over.

Finlay affectionately rustled the boy's mop of dark curls. "These scrapes on your knees and palms should heal fairly quickly." He eyed her. "What do you think, Cherub?"

"Aye, they'll heal within no time at all." She held Joseph's hands in hers as she looked into his wide brown eyes. "Why is it you allowed yourself to be taken by the MacKenzies?"

"I saw them in a vision. They wanted Mama." He sniffed and tried to hold back tears pooling in his eyes. "They knew she could take people backward and forward through time. I told them she couldnae anymore."

"You sought them out on purpose?"

"So they would leave." A tear slipped free and trailed through his dirt-smeared cheek. "Instead they took me and said they'd make certain Mama got her skill back."

"Oh, Joseph. I'm so sorry you've had to go through all of this." She held the boy close, rocked him gently against her chest. "You are as loyal and as protective as your mother is, but should you have another vision, you must tell her and your father all."

"I will." He wrapped his scrawny arms around her. "I'm so sorry."

"You're safe now, and that's all that matters." She kissed his damp cheek.

Kirk squeezed Joseph's shoulder then drew her back to her feet and into his arms. In her ear, he murmured, "He's well and now it's time to go home."

"Aye, home we shall go." She spread one hand over his heart. Her mate, the other half of her soul. He was a gift she completely adored and would keep safe, just as she kept her people safe.

Chapter 8

After returning to the castle and collecting Amelia and Olaf along the way, Cherub walked into the dark of her chamber as night fell. Such relief filled her. Her closest now remained safe behind these castle walls. Through her open window, moonlight streamed in and played over her golden canopied bed while a gentle breeze blew and lifted strands of her hair. All remained quiet within her element, no stirring of need from even one soul.

She stepped in behind her silk dressing screen propped in the corner, removed her gown and tossed it over the top. In her shift, she crawled into bed and rolled under the fur bedcovers.

"Cherub?" A rap sounded at the door. "It's Kirk. Can I come in?"

"Aye, of course." She'd left him below an hour ago while he'd been speaking with his brothers and Gilleoin. Plumping her pillow, she sat up as he strode in, his war coat and fur vest tucked over one arm and a traveling bag swinging from his hand. "Is all well?" she asked him.

"As well as can be. Gilleoin still has warriors patrolling the village and the coastline, and now an additional team have also been dispatched to the inn and will remain on alert there. If Colin MacKenzie makes a move, this time we'll surely see it." He closed the door, slid the bolt across and set his belongings on top of the wooden trunk near her window. With one brow lifted, he asked, "Have you had a chance to eat?"

"Aye, with Amelia and Olaf afore they tucked Joseph into bed. Nessa joined us. They'll remain here until the threat against them no longer exists." She plucked at the sheet draped over her lap. "Amelia asked me again if I can aid her in her retraining and I've given her my word I'll do so just as soon as possible. She must restore her skill, and to its strongest once more."

"That's great news." He knelt at the hearth, his white tunic stretched taut over his broad shoulders as he bent to the task of lighting the fire. Quickly and surely, he pulled stringy bark off a log, struck flint with his dirk then coaxed the sparks to life. He built a roaring fire with twigs and wood from the basket until the flames licked up the flue. Slowly, he rose, drew his shirt over his head and crossed to the side table. He unbelted his sword and weapons, propped them against the wall then poured water from the jug into the basin. Cloth dipped, he wiped his arms and chest, his golden skin gleaming in the firelight. His muscles bunched and moved as he bathed, every inch of his hard body making her fingers itch to touch him.

Heat flooded her below and she licked her lips, wishing she could lick him instead. "You are too far away."

"So are you." He dried himself, unlaced his boots then prowled toward her barefoot, his rawhide pants riding low on his trim hips. "Are you tired?"

"No' since the moment you walked in my door." She tugged the covers back on her side and wriggled over to make more room for him.

His golden gaze, so hungry and needy, devoured hers as he slid in beside her. "I'm a little worried you'll suddenly disappear again."

"I shall try to give you more warning the next time." On her side, she cupped his cheek and blew out a long breath. As much as she wished to complete the bond with him, one last glaring issue remained between them. "Kirk, I..." How did she word this?

"What's worrying you?"

"There is something we must discuss." She brushed her fingers back and forth over his stubbly jaw. "There is pain in living an endless life, and you're so very close to your brothers. Should we move forward with this bond, then you'll need to accept that one day they will age and pass away and you willnae."

"That thought crossed my mind, right after you told me Amelia spoke a spell to bind a piece of Olaf's soul to hers, that he too had now become an immortal as she was."

"Aye, they will walk the same path for the rest of their lives, together as one."

Looking into her eyes, he lifted a lock of her hair and twined it around his finger. "Which means I'll always be here on this Earth for my brothers, their children and their grandchildren and so on. That's a gift of reassurance I can give them, for all of us to treasure. As for the pain, I know the good times to come will far outweigh the bad and since we'll be able to travel through time, whenever I truly have a desperate need to be with them again, then it'll be possible to return to them. Won't it?"

"Aye, should you ever wish to see them, I will gladly take you to the time you need to travel to. I do so for myself with my own kin, so I need no' suffer too greatly either."

"See, then I'll never truly lose them and that in itself is yet another gift." He touched his heart. "So too, my brothers will always reside right here, where all my kin do, no matter where I am."

"As my kin do as well." Her heart lightened, the final fear which had been niggling at her winging away.

"There isn't anything we can't tackle, provided we do so together." He set one hand on her outer thigh, his warm palm like a brand against her skin. "We will always be one."

"All I want is to be yours, in every way." She spoke the words directly from her heart.

"As I wish to be yours." He eased her shift up until he'd exposed her entire leg then gently, he caressed her flesh, right over her thigh and around to her bottom. "Your skin is so soft, so dazzlingly bright even in the moonlight."

"If you find it too much of a distraction, I can cloak myself."

"Try it, and we'll be having words, harsh words." He leaned in and kissed her, his mouth moving over hers with a delicious demand that made her ravenous for so much more. "Cherub, I want to complete our bond and join with you in all ways. I long to form the merged link of the mind my shifter kind can, to speak to you at will, for us both to always know where the other is at any moment in time. I need that, and it can't wait any longer."

"I need that too. I also need to speak the spell to bind a piece of your soul to mine, so that I can keep you safe, from this moment forward and throughout all of time." She spread her hands over his wickedly wide chest. His warm flesh held a smattering of hair, the same glorious shade as his head, and his muscles, they rippled as she touched him, so strong and unyielding. He was all warrior, all man, and all hers. "There is no other for me, other than you."

"Aye, and no one can keep us apart, not even time itself." He dipped a finger along her shift's neckline. "I want to see all of you."

"Aye, please. I want that too." She couldn't halt her need, didn't have a chance of doing so."

"Arms up."

Slowly, she lifted them and he slid the white linen up and over her head. He tossed it aside, nudged her onto her back and with his gaze on hers, he traced one finger around her beading nipples. "Never did I ever imagine I'd be gifted with a mate such as you."

"Or I you."

"We'll remain together, from this moment forward. No one can ever separate us again." Gently, he eased her breasts together then dipped his head. The raspy stroke of his tongue across the sensitive tips sent a wicked bolt of pleasure straight to her core and he rumbled his pleasure, the vibration in his chest deep and throaty and giving evidence his bear sat close to the surface. "Me and my bear want to saturate you in our scent."

"Then you need to finish undressing." A trickle of hair narrowed down between his firm abs and disappeared below his waistband. She loosened the ties of his pants. "May I take these off?"

"Allow me." He seized the waistband and shoved the leather down his thickly muscled legs and off. One impressively large cock bobbed free and brushed his belly, the head a ripe raspberry color that made her mouth water for a taste.

She tip-toed her fingers down the long length of his shaft then brushed across the dark thatch of curls covering the apex of his groin. "From the moment you stood afore me on the beach, my desire for you rose and will now never abate. Thank you for coming for me, even though at first I chose to run."

"All I've wanted these past five years is to find you, to hold you in my arms and never let you go. Now that wish has come true." He knelt between her legs, his balls drawing firmer and higher, his shaft thickening and lengthening even further. "Although I do fear this night, and hurting you. It's the last thing I wish to do."

"I can handle a little pain. I'm also a woman who knows what she wants and that's not to wait another day until we join as one. I want you, and only you, for you to come deep inside me and join us together in a way I've never experienced afore."

"In a way I've never experienced before either, although I intend to see to your pleasure first." Licking his lips, he gazed at her below. "I'm also losing my mind right now at just the sight of you."

"As I've already lost mine." So many emotions tumbled through her, as well as a myriad of new sensations, all filled with longing, desire, and complete and utter need. She'd lived a lonely life, one mostly unseen, but she'd never need to remain that way with Kirk. She had opened her heart to him and now she intended to meld their lives together, in all ways. No more hiding. 'Twas time embrace her mate and her new future. "I want to touch you, just as you touch me, Kirk."

"I'm all yours."

"Aye, all mine." She stroked down his arms and over his sides then back up again, his body all superbly honed muscle and smooth skin. She cupped his face in her hands, ran her thumbs along his scrumptious lower lip, his warm mouth and hot gaze drawing her ever deeper under his spell. Completely breathless and a whole lot dizzy, she murmured, "I wish I'd known of our bond five years ago."

"Everything happens in its own time, and usually for a very good reason. At least now we need never look back but only forward." He swept his hands under her bottom, bent his head and pressed a soft kiss to her belly. "In order to complete the bond, we need to be skin on skin."

"Aye, I'm aware."

"Is there a chance you could conceive?"

"I've never aged past my twentieth year, not physically at least, so there is a chance, although a rather slim one. Due to my immortality, my courses fall years apart."

"Yet Amelia has given birth." He raised a curious brow.

"Aye. So too she's only conceived the once and she willnae have another chance to do so again until a new cycle begins. That could be in ten, twenty or thirty years from now. There's no telling when, only that it shall be quite some time away."

"You've known Amelia a long time?"

"Over a thousand years. She's been by my side, right through to the future. In truth, she found Olaf during a visit to the past only ten years ago, which is why she now lives here in this time. Joseph was born nine years ago, present, past and future included."

"I see." He smiled, although a look of longing still shadowed his eyes as he did. "I wish for children with you, at some point in time."

"Then you shall need to bed me, quite frequently, if you wish to ensure we're given the optimum chance for that to occur."

He grinned and kissed the tip of her nose. "That I can do. You mentioned when we met that Joseph too is an immortal. How is that possible?"

"Even though we can only spell one soul to ours, that of our soul bound mate, from the moment Joseph was conceived, his very soul became entwined with Amelia's in her womb through the natural bond of mother and child. That soul bond has never been severed or broken. In fact, their bond has only strengthened over the years."

"So any children we might have will be as you are, an immortal?"

"Aye, as we both will be."

"Then I give you fair warning." He touched his forehead to hers. "I intend for us to always be skin on skin. One day we'll raise a family of our own, children who'll travel through time with us. We'll have a whole tribe to aid us in doing your duty."

A depth of wonder filled her. 'Twas a dream she'd never considered. "Give me your promise that will be so."

"You have my absolute word, one which will always stand firm." He caught her hands, stretched her arms over her pillowed head and held them there. "Now, no moving for you. I want you to lie back, relax and think only of us soon being together and joined as we both desire. Although before that happens, I intend to taste every inch of you, to know your body as if it were my own."

"My body is already yours and was from the moment we met. I would never have been able to give you up, was a fool for thinking I could." She stretched and sank deeper into the mattress. "I want you, Kirk, all of you."

"Perfect, because I want all of you." Carefully, he raised her legs, hooked them over his shoulders until her bottom lifted off the bed and she lay fully exposed to him. His black hair became a silky brush against her skin as he lowered his head between her open thighs. "You're so pink and lush, beyond tempting and completely beautiful."

She'd never had a man so enraptured by her. "What are you going to do?"

"You should be asking what I'm not going to do." Grinning, he caressed along her inner thighs, parted her folds and slowly eased one finger deep inside her. The sweet invasion made her wriggle down to push his finger in further. "You like this?"

"Aye. There will be naught I willnae adore at your hand. That I can promise you. Your touch is sublime."

"Still, I want you to tell me what feels good and what doesn't. I only want to bring you pleasure this night." He stroked inside her harder and faster, then rubbed his thumb across her nub until she moaned in delight.

"That feels wonderful, but I need more," she panted.

"Like this?" He added a second finger then dipped his head and breathed in her scent. "Hell, you smell incredible, like the sweetest honey. I have to taste you, before my bear goes stir crazy." He licked her flesh then purred and dived in deeper. Thrusting his fingers so deliciously inside her, he kissed her in the most intimate of ways. Pleasure radiated through her core and rippled outward. She could barely keep still, her hips moving in a rhythm all on their own.

"Oh, sooo good." Her lashes fluttered down and she lowered her arms and cradled his head in her hands.

"You're a feast unlike any I've ever tasted." With deep and seductive strokes, he moved, every flick of his tongue and rub of his fingers making her gasp and move toward a peak that lay so temptingly close. Her desire built, higher and higher until she could barely hold onto any thought.

"Kirk." She needed to touch him too, desperately. Swiftly, she found the hard length of his cock then caressed his rigid flesh. He was so hot and hard and she wanted his shaft pushing deep inside her, as hard and fast as he could. "Please, kiss me. I want your mouth on mine and every inch of your body pressing down on me."

"I'm coming, my imp." He lifted up, took her mouth in a hot kiss even as he continued to rub his fingers over her nub so wickedly and wonderfully below.

"I need you inside me. I cannae wait any longer." An orgasm beckoned and she teetered on the very edge of a precipice she could barely hold onto.

"Are you sure you're ready?"

"More than ready."

"Then open wider for me." With his hands on her hips, he nudged his cock along her slick folds. With a delectably teasing smile on his lips, his gaze filled with desire, he rubbed his cock over her nub.

"Be mine," she whispered as something battered at her mind, demanding entrance.

"Always." He squeezed his eyes shut then grimaced as if in pain. "My mind demands the merged link."

"Then give it to me." She wrapped her legs around his waist and gripped his butt.

"I want you, only you, Cherub." He plunged inside her, tore through her barrier below and as he did, his mind barreled into hers as he joined them together, their minds and bodies as one.

So completely bare and open to him, she rejoiced as his mind tunneled deep inside hers and created a private pathway that would only ever be theirs. 'Twas the most stunning connection, one she grabbed ahold of and cemented within her own mind. Along the link, she whispered into his mind, *"There will be none who can ever part us, no' now."*

"You're my mate, the other half of my soul." He licked along her lower lip and liquid heat surged through her core. Then he deepened their kiss, so reverently, so breathtakingly.

"I feel so incredibly full, and also so at peace." Her heart and soul could barely contain the sheer depth of intense emotions rolling through her. *"I never want to let you go."*

"My search for you is done, and our life together can now finally begin." With his hands on the bed either side of her head, he eased back then carefully pushed all the way back in, right to the hilt. *"Hell, that feels phenomenal, like every inch of me is on fire and sparking where we touch."*

"You are right where you belong." Her lashes fluttered down.

"No, don't close your eyes. I love seeing you look at me." He increased his pace, moving deeper. *"I also want you to keep your mind open to mine, to let me see your thoughts so I can ensure your pleasure. It's my right to give it to you, and I intend to do so."*

"There's almost too much pleasure, yet I still cannae wait for more." She clung to him, her arms wrapped tightly around his neck and her legs firm around his hips as he thrust deep. He pounded into her and as he did, he laved the skin of her neck then sucked it between his lips. The thought of his bite sent such tortuously sweet sensations thrumming through her and when she shared them, he cupped the back of her head and brought her mouth to his neck.

"I want you to bite me, Cherub, the very moment I bite you, for us to always bear each other's marks."

"*I want that too.*" His enticing words had her rocking underneath him. She couldn't halt her body's need to move as one with him and when he scraped his teeth back and forth over her racing pulse, she did the same with him.

"*Do it, my love.*" He bit down and a fiery blast of pleasure consumed her.

Clasping him tight, she bit him in return and he roared his pleasure and plunged even deeper inside her, his pace feverish and his thoughts a whirlwind of pure heat blustering in and around her own. More, she wanted more, and so did he. She read it clearly in his mind. She clamped down on the other side of his neck and marked him again and he bit her hard and fast in return. She cried out at the intense joining, his bite making her channel tighten so exquisitely, and unable to hold on, she careened over the edge and flew to the stars, her inner muscles squeezing and dragging his cock to her core.

"*You're my mate, my lover, the other half of my soul.*" He bellowed and sank balls-deep inside her, his seed pulsing from him in one long hot stream that coated her womb. "*Speak the spell and ensure we're never separated again.*"

Aye, never would she allow a separation, not now. He would become an immortal as she too was. Looking deep into his eyes, she began, "From this moment forward, I hereby bind Kirk Matheson's soul to mine. Give me a piece of his inner light so that I might guide and watch over him, throughout all of time. He is mine, just as I am his."

A bright light shimmered from around his form and tendrils separated from his body and floated toward her. She breathed them inside her body and allowed the merging of all that they were, heart, body and soul. "No more separation," she whispered to him. "'Tis done. We are one, in every way."

"No more separation." He grinned and kissed her and she kissed him just as feverishly back.

* * * *

As he kissed his woman, Kirk locked his mind and body tight around Cherub's. So many intense sensations had stormed through him when she'd spoken the spell to bind his soul to hers. He'd even sensed the very moment when a piece of him had lifted free and been taken deep inside her. Then he'd cleaved to her and she to him.

"There's something I need to say," he murmured against her lips as he rocked gently inside her, as he attempted to bring them both back down from the heights they'd soared to. "I wish to reaffirm my vow to you. Cherub, from this day forward, I will honor your needs above my own, to give you what you so dearly desire and to ensure you never falter in your duty to your people. I also give you all that I am, my love and devotion, completely and fully."

"I have something to say to you as well." She caught his face between her hands and kissed him. "Kirk, from this day forward, I promise to keep your soul safe and to never allow another to harm you. I also give you all that I am, all my love and devotion. There is none other for me…other than you."

"Hell, I want to take you all over again." His cock stirred and lengthened inside her. "Only I don't wish to hurt you anymore than I already have." He pulled back and she tightened her hold around him, wrapping her legs firmer around his hips and her arms around his neck.

"No leaving me. I love the feel of you deep inside. You are where you belong."

"As I adore being right where I am, but I tore your maidenhead and I've a desperate need to ensure you are well. Allow me to take care of you." He eased from her and this time she allowed it, even though a tear leaked from her eye as he lifted free.

"It hurts to be apart." Her anguish at their separation pounded down their link toward him.

"I won't be a moment." It pained him as well, the wrench in

his chest a burning one. He rinsed out a cloth in the basin of water and tenderly wiped her clean. She enthralled him, from her wide blue eyes he wished to drown in, to her beautiful creamy skin that sparkled, and her addictive fresh scent he wanted to smother himself in.

"You've had your moment, Kirk. Come back here, now." She dragged him back to her and kissed him, all luscious pouty lips and soft murmurs as she demanded more of his exquisite touch.

Damn. It would be near impossible not to lose all control with her, to bury himself so deeply inside her he never emerged. "You must be sore."

"I'm in desperate pain. " Smiling, she pushed him onto his back and crawled on top of him, her glorious golden locks falling forward and sweeping across his chest. "Except for more of you. Now this is better. I can ensure you dinnae move away from me while I'm in this position on top."

"There are dark smudges under your eyes. You spent all night with me and didn't catch a wink of sleep. I should be taking more care of you." He swept her hair over her shoulders until every inch of her beautiful body was on stunning display. The way she straddled his hips and wriggled against his groin, her sensuous move making her slit rub the base of his erect cock wedged between them, was more than he could handle. He palmed her breasts, so heavy and full and completely impossible to ignore. "Lean forward, my love."

"As you wish." She eased forward and he grazed a finger from between her breasts to her belly then back again. Her breathing quickened and he lifted up a touch and captured one nipple in his mouth. He sucked the pebbled treasure deep inside his mouth then ever so gently, he stroked one finger through the golden curls covering her entrance and caressed her clit.

Squirming, she giggled. "Oh, that tickles. I'm feeling so sensitive right now."

She eased back and he lost his precious hold on her as she knelt between his legs, slid her hand around his cock and rubbed her breasts either side of his shaft.

"What are you doing?"

"I'm about to love you as you loved me." Peeking through her long lashes, she raised an alluring brow and the promise in her blue eyes sparkled with delicious intent. "Let me know if you dinnae like this."

Head dipped, she licked him in one long teasing stroke from base to flaring tip.

He groaned, long and low as he pushed against her for more. "I'll love anything you do, except I'm not sure how much of this I'll be able to handle."

"I need to touch you, just as you touched me." She cupped his balls, so softly, then caressing them, she settled her lips over his head and took him deep. A hot burn sizzled through his blood, all the way to his balls.

"Cherub." His cock went rock hard as her sweet mouth tortured him. She moved, her rhythm sheer perfection and her desire-filled thoughts rolling through his mind as she sent them winging toward him. She wanted to bring him to the brink of release just like this, right before he tasted her in the same way. Then she wished for him to thrust deep inside her channel below and make her fly.

She sucked him harder and he pushed deeper inside her mouth, until a sexual haze blurred his vision. She was a minx, and it was time to take back the control. He flipped her onto her back, planted his head between her thighs and grinned at the sight of her luscious pink folds lit a beautiful golden-red by the firelight. With her legs widened, he licked the plump nub awaiting his touch.

She gasped and wriggled. "I wasnae done."

"Too bad, because I have a bear greedy for more of you." With her clit between his lips, he smothered her in attention until she moaned and rocked her hips.

"I feel too much."

"So do I, and it's sheer bliss." He reached up and played with her nipples, the tips so incredibly pink and pointing upward. Needing another taste of those too, he rose up over top of her and devoured every lush inch of her breasts. He nipped and left his mark and she moaned for more each time he did, her back arching as she held his head to her breasts and pressed her nipples deeper into his mouth.

"Kirk, I want you inside me again. Dinnae deny me."

He couldn't, didn't have a chance of doing so.

His cock hammered at him for release and he grazed her hot flesh with his shaft, the head leaking pre-come.

"Aye, you're so close." She seized his butt, bucked against him and pulled him into her.

What his woman wanted was impossible for him not to give. She thrashed underneath him and his balls tightened and need pulsed. Crying out his name, she came, her inner muscles clamping down on him and he pounded into her and spurted his essence in one long hot rush. "You're mine," he whispered, "always mine."

"Aye, and never shall we be parted again." Her eyelids drifted down and she curled up against him and yawned. "I feel so sleepy."

"Then rest, my love. Sleep as long as you like. I'm not going anywhere and neither are you."

Sleep took her and gently, he tucked her against his chest, right next to his heart which would forever be hers. Beyond content with her in his arms, his soul bound to hers, he gave in and allowed sleep to claim him too.

Peace. The most incredible wave of peace washed through him.

Chapter 9

The chirping of birds and the warmth of sunlight drifted into Cherub's chamber and stirred her from her sleep. She stretched and caught her breath. Muscles not used before ached in protest, although the discomfort flittered away as the heat at her back and her mate's wonderfully spicy scent wrapped fully around her.

She wriggled around and faced him and he grumbled in his sleep, slid one muscled leg over hers to keep her in place then purred. His possessive hold made her pulse race, as did the sight of his jaw holding a dark razz of stubble and the wayward lock of inky-black hair curled cutely across his forehead. On one high cheek, a loose eyelash sat. She dabbed it with one fingertip, held it to her lips and gently blew on it. Swirling the air in the room, she sent his lash floating on the breeze, out the window and soaring high into the sky.

She dissolved into the air wad reappeared at the windowsill, swept the current carrying his lash ever higher then made a wish on it. "Please," she whispered, "aid me in ensuring all those who now sense the mated bond taking form, to find their chosen ones."

"Cherub." Kirk grumbled her name as he prowled toward

her. "Who said you could leave me?" He wrapped his arms around her from behind and crossed his forearms over her breasts. "You're also standing in front of the window where anyone might see you."

"There is no one about at the moment." Arms stretched high, she allowed the morning sun's golden rays to bathe her body.

"You're completely captivating with your sparkly skin and will draw attention in no time." He shuffled her to the side of the window, pressed her front against the wall and nuzzled her neck from behind her. He licked the mark he'd placed on the side of her neck, his erect shaft brushing her bottom. "Ignore that."

"There is naught about you I could ever ignore."

"Or I about you." He twirled her around, caught her up in his arms and walked with her to the golden curtained ambry. Once he set her back on her feet, he searched through her clothes, selected a gown and laid it on the bed. "You need to dress, and preferably before I end up tossing you back onto that mattress so I can have my wicked way with you."

"That was hardly a warning if 'twas your intention." She sidled up against him and his stunning golden eyes rimmed with a glimmer of starburst yellow devoured her.

"I want to eat you."

"That I would love."

"Cease tempting me. You'll be sore and you need some time to heal." He rubbed his body against hers, the fine dark hairs on his chest tickling her nipples and making them stiffen. Groaning, he threaded his fingers deep into her hair and played with the long golden blond strands. "My bear wants another taste of you."

"Your bear is welcome to taste any part of me he pl—"

He kissed her, deeply and wildly, until their breath mingled as one and completely scattered her thoughts.

"I, ah…" She shook her head to clear it. "My muscles ached

upon awakening, but those pains are now gone. There is no need to deny either of us what we desire."

"You're not being very helpful right now." He scooped a shift from the ambry shelf and slid it over her head. The thin white cotton slithered down her body and brushed her ankles. "I won't make you hurt any more than I already have."

"I truly dinnae hurt." She tip-toed her fingers down his chest and followed the thin trail of hair that passed between his abs and thickened into lush curls around his shaft. Gently, she cupped his balls and they tightened and drew upward. His cock lengthened and she encircled her hand around it. Looking into his eyes, she murmured, "Kiss me again."

"You need time to recover." He picked up her gown and over her head it went. She got a mouthful of cream silk before he swept in behind her and cinched the bodice's stays in place.

Burgundy ribbons fluttered from her waist as she spun about. "Now you'll just need to undress me again."

"I will, tonight, after you've had some time to heal." With a determined yet sinfully delicious look on his face, he picked up her gown's matching slippers from the ambry shelf and knelt at her feet. He lifted one foot, his hand roaming under her skirts and up her calf. She seized his broad shoulders and held on while he slid her slippers on. "I also need to talk with my brothers. Colin MacKenzie wanted a woman from the village, and from Joseph's account of his conversation with the warriors we fought, that woman was Amelia."

"Amelia is now safe."

"Amelia is also a time-walker, one of only two currently here in this time. You also popped up out of nowhere during the battle and our enemy saw you. Just like Amelia, you too need to remain well guarded."

"No one can capture or contain me, no' even you."

"There isn't a person alive who can't be held against their will." He cupped her face in his hands and kissed her. "Even you, my elusive imp."

"You are so frustrating." She crossed to the looking glass propped at the end of the side table against the wall and ran a brush through her hair.

"Keeping you safe is imperative." He collected his traveling bag from on top of the trunk and flipped open the leather flap. From within, he retrieved his clothes then donned a pair of black leather pants. He tugged his sturdy black boots on, strapped his sword belt and wrist daggers in place and eyed her. "I will always protect you, even from yourself if I must."

"'Tis also my duty to protect you."

"Which reminds me. You haven't actually explained exactly how my immortality now works. I don't doubt there will be another battle and I need to know specifics." Still shirtless, he strode to the side table and lathered soap in the basin of water. He smeared the bubbles along his jaw then slid his wrist dirk free and in the looking glass, bent to the task of shaving.

"Since I now hold a piece of your soul, you are as such an extension of me." Unable not to touch him, she ran her fingers through his silky shoulder-length black hair. "For as long as my heart beats, I can hold you to this Earth. I can also heal any wounds you might suffer from, in the same way I heal myself, including the soreness I had this morn. Each time I become as one with the air, when I reappear, each and every part of me is reformed. All wounds heal within the blink of an eye."

"How much energy does it take for you to transform me as you do yourself?" In a firm line, he ran his blade from his ear to his chin, first on one side of his jaw and then the other. His deft and precise strokes held her captive.

"You are a part of me now, just as I'm a part of you. To transform you as I do myself will take very little effort or energy."

"Show me." He faced her, held his blade to his bicep and sliced his skin. Blood flowed and rushed down to his elbow.

"Kirk, no!" She shimmered into air and took him with her then reappeared and grasped his arm. She wiped the blood away, the cut now gone. "Dinnae do that again." She slapped his chest.

"Tell me exactly how you fare." His mind moved through hers as he searched within her thoughts for an answer.

"I fare just fine." She huffed and paced the chamber. "That's if you ignore my now sudden bout of anger, which you shouldnae."

"I'm sorry. I didn't mean to upset you, but I had to check how this immortality now works." Facing the looking glass once again, he carefully swiped his blade down his neck and in the small space between his nose and lips then done, washed the remaining suds away. "Are you truly well?" he asked as he peered over his shoulder at her, concern deep in his gaze.

"No long-lasting harm can ever come to me. Rest is all I've ever needed to restore any lost energy." She scooped up a clean white shirt from his bag, returned to him and stroked down his healed arm. She'd make sure he never cut himself again.

"Do you feel well enough rested after last night?" He leaned his leather-clad butt on the edge of the side table, snagged her around the waist and tugged her in between his spread legs. "I kept you up for far too long."

"I am very well rested"—she hauled his shirt over his head—"although still mad."

"Then I'll just have to kiss you until your mad spell dis—"

A rap sounded. "It's Nessa. I ordered a tray and brought it up."

"Just a moment, Nessa." She freed herself from Kirk, unbolted the door and opened it.

Nessa bustled in wearing a forest-green gown and a white lace shawl, her red hair wisped with gray pulled back and contained within a low bun at her nape. She placed the tray on the table and glanced at Kirk. "Your brothers wished to see you. They both await you downstairs in the chief's solar with

Gilleoin."

"Then I'd best join them." He strode toward Cherub, his gaze a heated one as he caught her hands in his. "Don't remain mad at me for too long."

"Then dinnae cut yourself again. Go and join your brothers." She motioned toward the door.

"I'll go but only because I must." He popped a kiss on her forehead, swiped his deerskin padded cotun from his bag and strode out the door, his next words whispering through her mind. *"Just so we're clear, you're not to go anywhere without me. No rushing off to aid your kin unless you take me as well."*

"We shall see. Let me know how your meeting with Gilleoin goes." Yesterday when she'd spoken to Nessa about needing to ferret out information on Colin MacKenzie, she'd gotten sidetracked with meeting the ladies and then speaking with Kirk. Now, that need to find out exactly what Colin MacKenzie was up to, rolled through her with fierce strength.

"I mean it, Cherub. Where you go, is where I go."

"You need to have more faith in my abilities."

"I have the utmost faith in your abilities, but consider my request an order. I won't be parted from you, not for any reason."

"I have no' been ordered about in over a thousand years. I dinnae intend to be ordered about now." She plunked into the seat across from Nessa, her heart an aching mess as the distance between her and Kirk grew. *"I miss you."*

"I miss you, too."

"Are you well, my dear?" Seated, Nessa poured tea from the pot then nudged a cup toward her. "I'm always here if you need to speak."

"The mated bond is so very strong and illogically all-consuming. I must care for my people as needed, which I willnae be prevented from doing." Legs crossed, she selected an oat cake from the tray and munched on it. "Have you seen Amelia this morn?"

"She is breaking her fast with Olaf and Joseph in the great hall. Dinnae fear for them. They are here behind Gilleoin's walls and will remain so until all has settled and their safety assured. I also give you my word, that I'll remain alert for any visions, although there have been no more since the last regarding the MacKenzie chief. I certainly wish I'd had forewarning of Joseph's kidnapping."

"You cannae control your visions any more than I can control all that happens throughout time. People have freewill, and as such things are always in motion."

"Aye, we can only watch what we ourselves do and ensure the choices we make are sound." She lathered a slice of bread with raspberry jam and took a bite.

"Cherub?" Another knock. "It's Isla. Arabel's with me."

"One moment." With a swish of her silk skirts, she rose and opened the door.

Isla gasped, her gaze going wide and her jaw dropping. "Wow. Your skin truly does sparkle. Iain told me it was an incredible sight to see, and it surely is."

"Oh, how striking you are." Arabel clutched her cherry colored skirts and swept around her. "You're so wondrous to behold. Of course I've heard the firstborn within the royal line holds glittering skin, but to see it—well, this is a first."

"I'm also the last within the firstborn line to hold such skin, although I wish to be my true self amongst both of you and your mates." She motioned them toward the table. "Nessa and I were just breaking our fast. Have either of you eaten?"

"We've just done so in the great hall, although I'm still rather peckish." Isla bustled inside, pulled out a chair and sat before the table. "It seems I'm growing very hungry cubs."

"Then help yourself to whatever you wish." Cherub collected the corner armchair for Arabel and offered it to her. Arabel thanked her and sat.

"My hungry cubs seem to want an inordinate amount of meat right now." Isla selected a slice of bread and added a large wedge of beef and a sliver of cheese, her yellow gown with its long embroidered sleeves swaying gently over her wrists. She munched and moaned. "Mmm, this is just what I—they needed."

"Now that we're all here, I have good news I wish to share." Cherub picked up her tea cup and sipped the hot brew. "Last eve, I spoke the spell needed to bind Kirk's soul to mine. There is none now who can ever part us."

"That's the best news." Isla beamed.

"Oh aye, you have my most heartfelt congratulations as well." Arabel clapped. "I'm so happy for you both."

"Thank you, yet even in my happiness, I cannae forget that there remains a very real threat looming on the horizon. The Chief of MacKenzie intends to rule these waterways, and it appears he hopes to do so with the aid of a time-walker. Which means I need to know exactly what his coming plans are, then to halt him afore he can see to them. He must be stopped."

"I agree." Fire flared to life on Arabel's fingertips, her tone impassioned. "My apologies, but any talk of Colin MacKenzie always sets my anger to rising and fire to flaring. He cannae be allowed to harm anymore of our kin."

"I detest the man too, my dear, and you've no need to apologize." Nessa shuffled her chair closer to Arabel's and squeezed her granddaughter's shoulder.

"Then I shall leave immediately and ensure he cannae harm another soul." Cherub stood and glanced at Arabel and Isla. "When I am as one with the air, I can slip in and out of the smallest of spaces. I shall return once I know exactly what is going on."

"You must take care," Isla murmured as she rose to her feet.

"I shall." She melted into a mist and flowed out the open window. "*Kirk?*"

"*I'm here. Is something wrong?*"

"Nay, I just needed to hear your voice." Over the treetops, she soared then swept high into the sky, each breath she took coming harder and faster the farther she moved away from her mate. Pain lanced through her chest, so strongly and so swiftly she was forced to slow her ascent. The castle far below was a mere pinprick of gray amongst the jewel blues of the loch and the lush greens of the forest.

Confusion swirled through her mate's mind and raced along their link. *"I can sense distance between us. Where are you?"*

She rose through a layer of puffy white cloud, the air stirring and swirling all about. *"There are certain matters I must attend to."*

"We spoke about this. Where you go, is where I go."

"You're busy with your brothers right now and I didnae wish to take you away from them." She was also used to being alone. *"You must give me some time to accept all these new changes. I have acted alone for so long."*

Swiftly, she sped across the loch and along the land toward the northeast. Being as one with her element allowed her far faster movement, and right now, there could be no more delay.

"Soul bound mates should never be separated. We're a pair, best together and never apart. I'm here to aid you."

"You're right, although I'm almost where I need to be." She soared down through the sudden stillness in the air and skimmed the gray mist sitting low over the water, the fortified walls of the MacKenzie's keep shrouded within them. *"How are your brothers this morn?"*

"On edge now since I am. Tell me exactly where you are."

"The MacKenzie wants a time-walker, and I need to find out why. Until he is halted, Amelia and all those within the village remain in danger. That I cannae allow." She breezed over the foggy curtain wall and into the bailey. Below, men trained in battle leathers, dust pluming at their feet and mingling with the hazy air, their claymores clashing and each strike ringing loud in

her ears. Slowly, she circled the tower house then slipped inside the front door of the keep as a lad in breeches with suspender straps looped over his shoulders swept dirt from the doorway, outside.

"You're headed to the MacKenzie's lair?"

"Nay, I am already here." She sent a surge of warmth and love down their link, then whizzed through the hall holding three maids busily cleaning trestle tables before slipping underneath the chief's solar door and inside his inner sanctum. She'd visited this castle a number of times over the centuries, for one reason or another and as such knew her way about well enough. She breezed around the room holding an oak desk, a tall polished chest with a dozen or more drawers, and an armoire containing the chief's armor inside. At the narrow stained glass window overlooking the inner courtyard, she halted and drew her form back together. Cloaked and assured none beyond the window would be able to see her, she gripped the windowsill. Outside, fog swirled and the MacKenzie chief in his belted plaid appeared at the base of the stone stairs leading up to the barbican. He was unmistakable with his formidable size and grizzly features, his biceps bulging and legs almost as thick as tree trunks. *"I see Colin MacKenzie. Thankfully he's here and no' attempting to harm one of our own right now."*

"I'm on my way with my brothers. Stay hidden, Cherub. Don't let a soul see you."

"There is no need for you to set sail to these shores. I willnae be here long." She stepped across to the chief's desk where a quill and ink bottle sat between a pile of the seneschal's accounts and three rolls of parchment tied with red ribbon. Carefully, she unraveled the first roll and opened it. *"I'll do a quick search and see what I can discover. He intends to take control of Matheson land and I need to know how and why a time-walker is important to ensuring his ultimate plan is made successful."*

"Iain, Finlay and I are at the sea-gate."

"You dinnae need to come."

"You are mine to protect, and I'll do exactly that."

"What you are, is impossible." Now she was on a time limit. There was no way she'd allow her mate anywhere near the MacKenzie's heavily guarded keep. She scanned the first parchment holding dozens of names, all scrolling downward from two. Oh my. Her mother and father's names sat at the top of what was clearly a family tree. Each of their children's names written along with their offspring and so forth down the scroll.

"What's wrong, Cherub? I can sense the confusion in your mind."

"Colin MacKenzie holds my genealogy. I'm no' sure how he would have gotten this being that my kin reside beyond the veil." She continued to scan the names and tapped Samuel's name. Samuel, her youngest brother, had been the one to visit the village over two-hundred years ago. He'd fallen in love with the chief's daughter and wed her. There he'd lived, his line of descendants remaining strong at the village. She unraveled the other two rolls and frowned. Jeremiah and Amelia's ancestries were recorded on those. *"Kirk, there is more at play here than just the MacKenzie's desire to have a time-walker and to take Gilleoin's land. He has no' only researched my family line, but also Amelia and Jeremiah's. I'm missing something, although I dinnae know yet what."*

"Colin MacKenzie covets what he can't have. Consider that as you search for your answer."

"Aye, that he does." She returned to her own genealogy and straightened the bottom crinkly edge. In slanted script two words bloomed. Eternal life. *"Oh my, I've found the answer. The Chief of MacKenzie desires a time-walker in order to be as I am. He wishes for eternal life."*

A low growl rumbled from him. *"He's not going to get it."*

"Aye, 'tis impossible. Only you and those children born to

us can hold eternal life." She scrunched the parchment to her chest. *"He chases a dream that can never be."*

The door swung open and Colin MacKenzie barreled in, his gaze narrowing on the floating parchment. He slammed the door, seized the tartan blanket tossed over one of the armchairs and bunched it under the doorway. Rising to his towering height, he muttered, "Well, well, well. Who do we have here?"

Heart thumping, she dropped the parchment and it toppled to his desk and rolled off the side. Damn it. She'd never been caught unawares like this before.

The MacKenzie heaved his heavy armoire in front of the door and fully blocked her exit out. "My spies have informed me that Amelia and her kin are under heavy guard at Matheson House, so that must mean the unseen visitor in my solar must be the faerie king's daughter herself, the one they call Cherub, the one my men saw appear out of thin air as they fought the 'power of three' at the inn."

She swished to the window, scrambled to find an opening but the decorative stained glass was firmly fixed in place. She spun about. There wasn't even a fireplace that she could use to breeze up the flue. Never had she been trapped in such a way. Teeth gritted, she faced her adversary. "No one can capture or contain a time-walker, no' even you."

"Yet it appears as if you're now contained." Prowling the solar, he waved his hands through the air in search of her. "During the last Twelfth Night and Yule celebrations, I met a bard who had spent a great deal of time at the fae village. He recited an interesting tale of the time-walkers to me, then he aided me in compiling what he'd learnt from the villagers themselves."

"Your records are inaccurate."

"I dinnae believe so." He rubbed his callused hands together. "Amelia is of an endless age and so too is her mate, a man who is naught but a fisherman, a man she fell in love with ten years ago then spelled to her."

"*Cherub?*"

"*I'm here, and I'm—*"

MacKenzie lunged and she dissolved her cloaked form, swept up and floated along the low ceiling.

"*—fine. Just peachy-fine, my bear. How's your journey across the loch faring?*"

"*We've just hit the mist shrouding the MacKenzie's lair.*"

"You cannae escape me now, princess." The chief shoved the tall polished chest in front of the decorative window and blocked the meager light filtering in from it. A shuffle and scrape sounded in the near dark then a candle flickered to life on the corner of his desk. He tucked his dirk and flint away then swept the candle around the solar as he scoured the room for her.

"*Cherub, why can I sense fear ricocheting down our link from you?*"

"*'Tis good to know the mist remains thick. Dinnae let any of the guards see you scale the curtain wall. That is the only way in since this castle is built on a rock a hundred feet from the shore. There are most certainly men positioned on the battlements on the northern side. Please take care as you wander around and about.*"

"*You're actually encouraging me to storm the castle?*" His confusion swarmed through her then his worry roared to life. "*What the hell is going on? Tell me you're all right.*"

"*I'm sorry, but I'm in a spot of trouble.*"

"*I'm coming. Hold tight.*"

* * * *

Cherub's words reverberated through Kirk's mind and made his heart lose one very necessary beat. Through the cloying mist, he eyed his brothers. "Cherub's in trouble."

"What's happened?" Iain lowered the skiff's limp sail, the steady wind that had brought them across the channel having died away as they'd neared the calmer waters surrounding the

MacKenzie's keep.

"MacKenzie is after eternal life, except Cherub can only bind her mate's soul to hers and that of any children she conceives." He nabbed the oars, sat on the center bench seat and rowed. Finlay grabbed a second set of oars and rowed from the seat behind him.

"Hell, he's a nasty piece of work." Iain spat the words out as he gripped the rudder and searched through the gray haze to keep them on course. The curtain wall appeared out of the soupy gloom, just twenty feet ahead.

"She said there are guards on the northern side." Kirk stowed his oars and as the hull scraped the ground underneath the water, he bounded out onto the sliver of stony land encircling the keep. With his hands fisted on his hips, he took in the massive stone wall that rose into the fog high above.

Iain secured their skiff to a boulder and patted the wall. "It's slick with moisture but there appear to be plenty of hand and foot holds. We'll be able to scale this."

"Who's going first?" Finlay tucked his loose blue shirttail into his black pants, his ever-present sword at his side as he moved in next to them.

"Not Iain, not when he goes regimental in a kilt." Kirk grasped the wall and swung up, his booted feet wedged in the footholds. Getting to Cherub as quickly as possible, drove him forward.

"Hey, Isla never complains about me going regimental." Iain gripped the grooves and climbed up in his wake.

"Flipping, flapping kilt." Finlay groaned and clambered up after them. "I should have moved faster. The mist is not thick enough to cover your unmentionables, Iain, which are just about right in my face."

Iain chuckled. "You're just jealous."

"You wish," Finlay shot back at him. "By chance did you tell Isla what you're up to right now? Because I bet those unmentionables of yours won't get some use for some time if you didn't."

"Ha. If I told her where I was or what I'm doing, she'd be out the door, on a skiff and over here in less than a second. There is no halting a compeller from joining a battle when it looms." Iain grunted as he climbed. "What she doesn't know, can't hurt her. Or at least that's what I'm hoping."

"This is just like the old days." Pride filled Kirk's chest as his brothers followed right on his tail. They would never allow him to lose his woman, would always be right at his side no matter what battle he faced. "You're both ready to catch me in case I fall, right?"

"If you fall, I'm letting you whizz right on by." Iain swung up beside him. "You are the only one of us right now who can handle any drop. You should fall back below Finlay there and get ready to catch either of us if we fall."

"Would you two quit yacking and get to climbing. Fierce warriors await us and I need to get myself pumped up for a fight." Finlay swung wide and scrambled past Iain. "Last one to the top has to explain all this to the women once we return."

They all picked up their pace, using whatever crack or ridge the wall offered.

Determined to get to his woman, Kirk reached the top first, hauled himself over the edge then leaned over the crenellation and gave Iain and Finlay a hand each and swung them in beside him. As three, they crouched on the rampart, the mist thick and steady around them with not even a tiny breeze to stir the air. *"We're here. Where are you, love? And be exact."*

"In the chief's solar. Ground floor, first door on your left just off the great hall. There were three maids clearing the tables when I arrived, and one lad sweeping the area, but they were almost done." A wealth of worry channeled through from her. *"I'm in mist form and can remain this way for as long as it takes, but the MacKenzie's with me and he's barricaded the door and*

the window. There's no way for me to escape until there's a sliver or gap for me to breeze through. Did I mention I missed you? Because I really do."

"*I miss you too, and I'm coming to get you.*" He crept toward the stairs leading downward and motioned his brothers to follow. "She's in the chief's solar with the chief, ground floor, first door on the left. The hall should be clear, for the most part."

"Sheesh. The chief's solar?" Iain blew out a long breath. "Your woman clearly likes excitement."

"Aye, it seems my woman is no different to either yours or Finlay's." If Isla and Arabel were here right now, they'd for sure be right in the thick of things. Kirk halted at the base of the stairs. Across the yard, a good twenty warriors trained, their swords clanging loud with each hit. Great, that was about twenty more warriors than he wanted to see right now.

"We're clearly going to need a plan if we wish to get inside without being seen." Finlay gestured toward the pathway that led around the tower house toward the heavily paneled front doors with its thick iron scrollwork. "It's a small walk, but an immensely viewable one all the same. There must be a window open somewhere we can slip inside instead of taking that route."

"I don't have time to find an open window. We're walking right along that path, as if we're meant to be here." Kirk slapped Finlay on the back. "Try and cover Iain if you can. Regimental and wearing the Matheson plaid. He's got 'come-and-fight-me' written all over him."

Hand firm on the hilt of his belted sword, Kirk strode toward the front door.

"Thanks, little brother," Iain muttered as he jogged in beside him. Finlay caught up and stepped in on Iain's other side to cover him from sight.

"Any time." Kirk walked through the front door. A maid with an armful of tankards bustled toward the kitchens at the far side of the great hall and disappeared.

Iain snagged a folded tartan from a pile of clean MacKenzie plaids on the table underneath their hefty clan shield and wrapped it around his waist. "Right, let's get your woman and then get out of here."

"That sounds like the perfect plan to me." Kirk stepped up to the chief's solar door. "*Cherub, we're here. Right outside the door. On the count of three, we're coming in.*"

"*He's armed, Kirk, with a claymore holstered across his back and an axe at his side. Wrist daggers too. The armoire looks heavy, and it's right in front of the door. I'll divert him as well as I can. Be careful.*"

"*I will. Steer clear of the door.*" He eyed his brothers and repeated Cherub's words. Through good times or bad, no matter what difficulties they faced, they always stood as one. "On the count of three, we bust this door down. Ready?"

"Aye, 'the power of three' aren't complete until we have all our women with us." Iain swung his sword free. "Three," he bit out.

"Two," Finlay muttered and heaved back one step.

"One." Kirk nodded at his brothers, his blood roaring for revenge. No one would capture and contain his woman, not while he still had breath.

Chapter 10

Cherub rushed through the air toward the far side of the solar and shimmered into view. She held a piece of Kirk's soul deep inside her and she would fight the enemy for her freedom, just as her mate intended to fight for hers.

Colin MacKenzie sneered and stormed toward her, victory sparking in his gaze. He snatched her arms and hauled her up against him. "I want eternal life, and you're going to damn well give it to me, right n—"

A crash sounded. The door splintered and the armoire toppled over. Kirk and his brothers jumped the debris, their swords raised. MacKenzie dragged her in front of him and slid his blade hard up against her neck. "Dinnae come any closer," he snarled at Kirk.

"Well, unless you wish to lose your head right now, you'll release my mate." Biceps bulging, his gaze fierce, Kirk stormed toward her.

"She has no' taken a mate, and I intend to be the one that she does." MacKenzie's fetid breath washed over her face. "Speak the spell to bind us, princess."

"I'm no' your princess and I've already spoken the spell with the man who stands afore you. He is my chosen one, just as

I am his." She cocked a brow at Kirk. "I wish to leave. Are you ready to go?"

"I won't be a moment. No one raises a blade to my woman without learning a very strong lesson, that it'll never happen again."

"Those there are fighting words," the MacKenzie spat at him, his voice rumbling low and deadly. "But I hold her and you dinnae."

Goodness. She needed to get out of the middle of this fight. As one with the air, she disappeared and swirled in behind Kirk before retaking her true and visible form. With one hand against his back, she breathed in a rush, "I'm right here."

"Iain, watch Cherub for me." Kirk let out a fierce battle cry, one that rang in her ears then echoed out into the hall.

MacKenzie came at Kirk, just as Kirk came at him.

Their two great blades clashed dead center and sparked, the brutal force of the strike sending Kirk lurching back a step under the jarring impact.

"There is naught I like more than an eager opponent." MacKenzie slid his axe free, both his weapons in hand.

"I'm the most eager opponent you'll ever meet. Let's end this." Kirk struck and MacKenzie lunged and met his attack.

"You'll never halt me from getting what I want." MacKenzie grinned as the clamor of booted feet traveled toward them.

"Damn, it looks like we're about to have company." Iain bounded over the splintered armoire and into the hall. Cherub rushed in behind him. A wall of oncoming warriors loomed, their weapons raised. "Finlay, Kirk," Iain bellowed. "We need to leave, now!"

"Give me one more moment." Kirk slammed his blade into MacKenzie's, so hard the man tumbled to one knee. Finlay whacked MacKenzie's axe from his hand and Kirk slid his sword tight against their enemy's throat and pressed until blood oozed.

"Never, ever, touch my woman again, or next time I will slice your head from your shoulders. Eternal life will never be yours, not so long as I live."

MacKenzie opened his mouth to answer but Kirk smashed the hilt of his sword down on his head and he slumped onto the ground.

Kirk leapt out the door, Finlay right behind him and never had she been more proud of her mate. Or more worried.

"Hold onto me," she yelled to Kirk and his brothers.

They all snatched ahold of her then she did as she was born to do, her duty, that of protecting and guarding her kin. With a flick of her fingers, she swirled the thick air in the hall into a twirling mass and sent it whirling into the oncoming warriors. They skidded backward and toppled over each other. They tumbled out the wide open double doors and across the stony yard.

Outside, the mist rose with the rush of wind that she continued to churn and swiftly, she followed her enemy, the 'power of three' connected to her and kept safe within the cocoon of stillness she maintained around the four of them. In the center of the courtyard, she shouted over the melee, "I am Cherub, and from this day forth, should you ever think to attack my kin again, I will bring the wrath of the skies down upon you until not one stone in this keep stands."

"Well said." Kirk tightened his hold around her waist from behind. "And remind me to never rile you up in the future."

"Aye, I wouldnae recommend it." She smiled at him, cloaked them all then swept them up into the sky and over the curtain wall before lowering them gently down onto the rocks next to their skiff. She patted her racing heartbeat. Never had she placed herself in such a dire position before.

Kirk scooped her up into his arms, crushed her against his chest in a fierce hold and kissed her. "You're not to leave me again, and I want your word on that."

"Aye, I can see the benefits to keeping you close." She kissed him back, just as fiercely as he'd kissed her. She'd never leave on another mission of such importance without him at her side and she sent that promise winging down their link directly to him.

"Good. I'm glad we're finally in agreement."

"Aye, in agreement, but I still intend to keep you on your toes. That too I give you my word on."

"Somehow, I don't doubt you will." Breathing heavily, he stepped into the skiff, sat at the stern and with her cradled in his lap, eyed his brothers. "I'll clearly need aid from you both over the coming years. Being mated to a time-walker will likely hold its thrills and spills."

"Finlay and I will always be here for you." Iain released the mooring rope. "It appears there's no taming any of our women. We're all in for a very exciting life."

"A life I can't wait to live." Finlay raised the sail, a teasing grin on his face as he glanced at Cherub. "Dear sparkly sister, please rustle us up some wind. It's time to go home."

"Of course." Grinning back at him, she flicked her fingers and sent a whoosh of wind slapping into the sail.

As they sped back across the loch, she snuggled deeper into Kirk's embrace and nuzzled his neck. Aye, there was definitely no taming her, not when all she wished was to offer her people all her love and aid. Her mate now as well.

She smiled and kissed the man her soul rejoiced at being as one with. For him, her love and aid would always be endless, just as the streams of time she traveled were.

* * * *

Later that evening after transporting herself and Kirk to the future and to a place she held dear to her heart, Cherub sighed with heartfelt relief as she walked into her chamber on the uppermost floor of her home overlooking Angel Bay. 'Twould be just the two of them here in her keep high on the cliffs until they needed to return once again to the past and to his brothers.

She worked the back stays of her gown loose then wriggled the cream silk down past her hips and to the floor. She folded her gown on top of the elegant royal-blue padded wingback chair she'd purchased in the nineteen-hundreds. This modest castle was filled with treasures she'd collected over the centuries, a home she would now gladly share with her mate. Aye, never again would she be alone.

"I wish I'd known this place was yours." Kirk opened the stylishly stained glass doors leading onto her balcony and hooked them back to allow the fresh breeze in. In the doorway, he stood as he gazed out at the night sky. "I've scoured that bay below for you many a time. In fact on my very first visit here I met an old man walking along the beach who lived on this property. He assured me there were no women living within."

"That will be Gerard, and he's rather protective of me. He's one of my great-great, well there are a fair number of 'greats' in there, nephew. He lives in the cottage beyond the gardens and oversees all. I also keep a minimum of staff on hand. Close kin, all of them, and as trustworthy as can be, two maids and a gardener included. They have rooms below on the first floor."

"Then you'll need to introduce them to me."

"I shall, although no' this eve. Tonight is our night and no others'." Wind rustled the thick burgundy velvet drapes hanging either side of the door. She tied them back with the gold-tasseled ties and wandered onto the balcony. With her arms raised, the wind whispered across her skin and flapped her shift about her legs. As the air swirled, so too did it bring with it the promise of all the future held. Souls had been bound across time and her kin now awaited her aid in bringing them together.

"Can you sense anything?" Kirk brushed in behind her, the warmth of his chest against her back sublime. She leaned back against his heavenly hold.

"There are many now in need of my aid, both from yours

and Murdock's clan. Their mates reside in the past, their women awaiting them." Far below, moonlight played over the white-capped waves of Loch Shin as they tumbled into shore, and high in the night sky, a myriad of stars twinkled within the heavenly blanket of midnight-blue. She turned in Kirk's arms and wrapped her hands around his neck. "The 'power of three' will be needed both here in the future and of course in the past. I sense that, strongly, although 'tis hard to explain the how and why of it, just that it is what will be."

"Iain and Isla, and Finlay and Arabel won't have any issue with you taking us wherever we're needed, from the past to the future, or anywhere in between. Our mission won't be complete until all of our clansmen find their chosen ones. Do you have the names of those who are newly soul bound, who we'll soon need to find and offer our aid to?"

"If I did, and if I told you, would you be able to keep their names to yourself?"

"Hardly. If I can help them track down their chosen ones all the quicker, then I will."

"Yet a mated man actually longs for the chase, and part of his journey is in what he must overcome in order to be with his chosen one. That journey builds the foundation for their bond and all that 'twill be. I happily bring them to the right place and time, but that is all. You wouldn't wish to deprive your clansmen of the chase that awaits them, would you?"

"When you put it like that, perhaps not. Although if you truly wish to persuade me to your way of thinking, then you'll need to distract me from my good intent."

"And I believe I know just the way." With a teasing smile, she slunk backward into her room and crooked a finger. "Except right now, you're far too overdressed for the distraction I have in mind."

"That sounded like a dare, and I do love a dare." Stalking her, he unstrapped his weapons, laid them on the trunk at the end of her four-poster bed then tossed his rawhide jacket on top and kicked off his boots. He stood in his black leather pants and white shirt, the crystal-beaded chandelier overhead casting its golden glow over him. "I need you, bad."

She reached up on her toes and kissed his chin. "And you're still far too overdressed. Take your shirt off."

"Your wish is my command." He gripped the hem of his billowy shirt and hauled it over his head.

Warm golden skin shone and she stroked his wide chest and shoulders. "You're so beautiful, if one can call a warrior that."

"Call me whatever you wish, but I'm one warrior who needs to make love to his woman, right here in this bed, or anywhere else that might take your fancy or mine."

"I have a fancy for everywhere." She traced the tip of his cock attempting to spear through his black leather pants. Gently, she worked the leather ties loose, wriggled them down his legs and on her knees on the plush white bedside rug, grasped his cock with one hand and palmed his balls with the other.

His breath whooshed out, and he arched into her. "When you touch me like that, everything feels so sensitive."

"Just as I feel when you touch me." She licked him from root to tip. "Touching you like this also makes my nipples harden and heat flood me below."

"Now you're the one who's by far overdressed." He lowered and knelt in front of her, seized her shift's hem and tugged it over her head. Caressing her breasts, he swiped his thumbs over her beaded nipples. "So beautiful. I've missed the taste of you, although if I go too fast right now then tell me. I can barely contain my need, or my bear's. He's ravenous for more of you."

"I dinnae mind fast or slow, no' when we have the entire night ahead of us, and an entire lifetime too." She toppled him back onto the rug and slid over top of him. She swept her tongue inside his mouth and kissed him, until his breathing became as ragged as hers and the very air around them thickened with a pounding heat. The bed could wait. She wanted him right here, right now. "I'm so incredibly hungry."

"As am I." He rolled her onto her back, dipped his head and sucked her nipple deep inside his mouth. He played the tip to perfection with his tongue before moving to her other breast.

"Mmm, I love it when you touch me like this."

"I'm sure I love it more. Are you ready for a coupling like no other?" He spread her legs, pure need lacing his tone as he bent and nuzzled the inside of her thighs. His nose brushed her nub and he breathed deep, groaned and plunged his fingers inside her. Licking her most private place, he caressed her with his tongue, so seductively, so deliciously.

Desire swarmed her and she widened her legs farther as he loved her with such heart-pounding intensity. Need consumed her and her desire soared to such a thunderous level she couldn't help but cry out his name. "Kirk, I need it hard and fast, with you inside me. Slow can come later."

"Hard and fast it shall be." He flipped her over onto her hands and knees on the rug, his cock rising higher and firmer as he crowded her from behind. The fiery heat of his chest on her back as he rubbed against her made her throb for more. "Are you ready?"

"More than ready." She smiled back at him, her hair sliding off her back and over her shoulder. "Take me."

"You never need ask me twice." He opened her folds and with one finger stroking along her slit, scraped his teeth along her neck.

"Are you going to bite me too?"

"Aye, and far more than once before this night is through." He clasped her hips, pushed his cock between her legs and before she could draw her next breath, he plunged inside her.

He took her just as she'd asked, his mind locked tight around hers as he shared his pleasure and she shared hers with him in return. Then he bit down on her neck and she pushed her bottom into his groin. Each time he thrust forward, she met his move and urged him deeper. Her passion soared from the dual sensations of his possession, both body and bite, her inner muscles clamping down on him. Untold pleasure barreled through her. Never had she ever expected to be gifted with such an incredible soul bond as this. *"I love you, Kirk, and all that you are."*

"As I love you. You'll always be mine, just as I'll always be yours, and no one shall ever tear us apart." He plunged balls-deep inside her, his seed shooting to her core.

Heart pounding, she flew over the edge and joined him in heaven, her inner muscles gripping him tight.

Aye, they had an eternity together, a treasure of time she'd never relinquish. He'd found her, and she'd found him, and together, they would always be one.

* * * *

Never had such a wildly desperate need to mate ever consumed Kirk. Cherub pulsed around his cock as she tugged him ever deeper inside her heat. She was the only woman he'd ever desire, the only woman who would ever hold him, heart, body, and soul. She was his sanctuary, his home, his everything and all.

Bringing them both gently back down, he slowed his rocking then withdrew from her. Not for long though. He scooped her into his arms and carried her into her bathroom connected to her chamber. After flicking on the overhead light, he strode across the gold and cream floor tiles, set her down then opened the glass shower door and flicked the lever up. He'd missed the conveniences of his time while in the past, or at least a little bit. Hot water on tap had been one of those conveniences. He stuck his hand under the flow, waited for it to hit the perfect temperature then swept his woman inside with him and closed the door.

On the wall across from them hung a massive mirror, one which reflected Cherub's luscious body, from her rounded bottom to her long golden locks that tumbled to her waist. Her sparkly skin gleamed and the sinfully sexy sight had him aching to be inside her all over again.

"I'm going to be rather insatiable for a while." He looked deep into her divine blue eyes. "Can you handle that?"

"I've waited over a thousand years for you. I'm going to be rather insatiable myself for a while." With one hand on his chest, she pushed him against the glass wall, curled her other hand around his nape and with the shower water sluicing down their bodies, brought his mouth to hers and kissed him with a ravenous hunger that matched his own.

Hot water pummeled them and she hooked one leg behind his knee and rubbed up and down his calf. The delicious sensation of her smooth skin against his hairier body had his bear clawing for more. "There isn't any part of you I don't absolutely adore and I can't wait to sample more of you."

"Then sample away, because I intend to do the same with you." She rubbed her breasts against his chest then leaned in and sucked on his neck. His cock stiffened even further and his spine tingled as the pressure in his shaft built, so swiftly, so surely.

"We might need to do hard and fast again. I have next to no control right now." He grit his teeth in an attempt to hold off the sheer pleasure racking through him but to no avail, not when she grasped his cock and worked him in long pulls.

"Make us one, Kirk. There is no need to wait." She wrapped her arms around his neck and with the water's heavenly steam swirling around them, he cupped her bottom and did exactly as she'd asked. He lifted her up, dropped her down on top of him then pumped into her, his mind becoming lost within hers as he took her just the way they both needed, the way their bodies strived for and together, they rose to a great height before soaring to the very stars themselves.

Aye, there would be time for a slow loving at some point. He'd make certain of it. She was his, the only one he'd ever desire and he would savor every single inch of her over every single day to come. Such peace invaded his soul. No more searching. He'd found his chosen one, a most wondrous and loving woman who matched him in every way, to the depths of his soul.

Chapter 11

Warm summer-kissed morning air breezed into Cherub's chamber through her open balcony doors and swirled around her. She lay with her head nestled against Kirk's chest, his arm wrapped tight around her waist and his breath fanning her cheek. The crashing of the waves far below on the beach and the seagulls squawking over something they'd clearly found of interest made her smile. She loved being at home, but even more than that, she loved lying next to her mate. With her heart filled with love, she lifted up and gazed at him then holding perfectly still, embedded the moment deep into her mind.

Kirk's long black lashes swept low over his high cheeks, his lips lifted contentedly in sleep. After their shower, he'd made love to her four more times, his shifter ability giving him an increase in stamina she completely adored.

Softly, she kissed his closed eyelids, his cheeks and nose sprinkled with freckles, all while the wind whispered across her skin and spoke to her very heart. She stopped and frowned as a trace of need suddenly rippled toward her.

Isla and Arabel. The clergyman had arrived at the keep.

"Kirk?" She kissed his lips and he stirred. "We need to return to the past."

"This very minute?"

"Aye."

"Is there a reason for the hurry?" His arms banded tighter about her as he opened his beautiful golden eyes.

"Isla and Arabel spoke to Nessa a few days ago and Nessa sent a guard to fetch Father John from the priory. The ladies wish to wed their mates although your brothers know naught about their plan to do so. 'Tis a surprise, which means we must leave now so I can add to their special day with a surprise of my own. I wish to collect some very special guests along the way." She became as one with the air and breezed to her wardrobe door then retook her form.

"Cherub," he grumbled and slapped the mattress. "I really hate it when you flitter right out of my arms like that."

"I'm sorry. I shall try to remember not to do so." Smiling, she walked into her walk-in closet. Clothing to suit the ages hung clean and pressed by her maid, from jeans, sweaters, skirts and day dresses, to silk and satin gowns in an array of glittering colors.

She selected a gown of cream and gold silk, one with long lacy sleeves that fluttered to her fingertips. With the mountainous folds of fabric in hand, she eased the material over her head and the soft layers whooshed down her body. She laced the bodice's front stays, slid on a pair of matching slippers then strode into her bathroom and brushed her locks.

"You are moving far too fast." Kirk still lay in bed, his arms crossed behind his head as he watched her through the open doorway between them.

"Oh, I completely forgot. You'll need clothes too and you dinnae have any here." She walked to the bed.

"I'm certainly a little short on clothes at present." He shoved the golden covers back and stood, every inch of him so deliciously nude. Gently, he reached out a hand and curled one of her blond locks around his finger. "You look beautiful,

Cherub, and I'm the luckiest man on this Earth to have found you."

"Lucky, yet still nude." She caught his hand and kissed his palm. "Even though I've been to Ivanson Castle afore to visit one of your clansmen, I've no' actually been to your chamber. Show me an image of it in your mind so I can travel straight there. I'll gather some clothing for you and return as quickly as I can."

"You're welcome to the image in my mind, but you're not leaving me behind. I'll wear what I've got until I can change." He frowned as he eyed her. "Exactly which one of my clansmen have you already visited?"

"Dr. Tavish. I had a need to take one of my wounded kin from the past to him, for an ailment that required a certain degree of his special twenty-first century care. A couple of follow-up visits were included."

"Tavish is my second cousin. He and Tor, his brother, are identical twins. Neither have ever sensed their mates, and both came of age around the same time as me and my brothers did." He picked up his discarded clothing from the day before and donned the leather pants and now crinkled shirt. With his weapons in hand, he wrapped one arm around her waist. "Who are the very special guests by the way?"

"Your parents and Isla's father. I cannae allow either Michael and Megan, or Murdock to miss their children's wedding day." She nabbed the image of his chamber from his mind and focused on it. The air swirled as she opened a portal. It tunneled around them and then they fell away into the dark abyss, both holding onto each other.

Moments later she arrived in Kirk's chamber and the air settled. His large bed with its thick black fur bedcover and plump white and black striped pillows dominated the room. In the corner a tall chest with glass fronted doors showcased a collection of ancient weaponry within, from dirks to swords to war axes, while on the wall near his bathroom door a glorious family portrait hung.

Taken by the image, she walked across and stroked one finger along the lower wooden edge of the frame. Iain and Finlay stood impeccably attired in black dress pants and collared shirts, each standing either side of their mother seated on a roped swing under the shade of a golden-leafed tree. Kirk and his father stood behind Megan, both with a hand on her shoulders. **Megan's black wavy hair swished about her shoulders in a soft bob and her beautiful smile lit up her face.** She'd seen his parents from afar during those flying visits to Dr. Tavish, so she knew exactly who they were.

"I love this portrait." Kirk brushed in behind her. In the image, Michael's hair was the same midnight-black shade as his sons' hair, although it held just a sprinkle of gray at the sides. "They completed the bond right after they came of age, and my brothers and I were born exactly nine months afterward."

"You were all clearly eager to enter the world."

"Very eager, and now I know why. You were already waiting for me." He kissed the top of her head then strode to his wardrobe and pulled down a canvas case from the uppermost shelf. He popped the case on top of his bed and added clothes from his oak dresser—shirts, pants, casual jeans and jackets.

"I would have waited for you forever." She blew him a kiss.

"I'm glad you did." He ambled into his bathroom with its sandy and cream colored décor, then rummaged through a drawer and withdrew his shaver. A gentle hum buzzed as he shaved.

Smiling, she crossed to his window, parted the white drapes and opened the window a notch. Fresh pine air breezed in from the thick forest all around.

Below in the stony inner courtyard, muscled men trained in white shirts and belted Matheson plaids, each strike of their blade against the other's ricocheting toward her. The two

Matheson clans here in the future, both Kirk's and Murdock's across the other side of the Highlands, reveled in keeping to the old ways even though they lived in modern times. With their increased shifter strength, the men also required intense training in order to expend their abundant energy.

Eyes closed, she raised her arms and the wind whispered across her skin and with it brought the call of those unmated males below. Here, in this place with them, their need rang stronger. Aye, so many would need to travel to the past, and she wouldn't rest until each and every man had found his chosen one. Both of the Matheson clans' numbers had dwindled over the centuries until they'd neared extinction, but no more. Times were about to change, and would bring with it a new and wonderful future they'd all welcome with open arms.

"You look happy." Kirk walked toward her, now clean shaven and his hair combed. He'd donned an impeccable blue dress shirt and tucked it into a pair of pressed black pants.

"I'm in heaven now I have you to aid me in my duty." She shared her thoughts as he stopped before her then she reached up and straightened the collar of his silk shirt. "You look so handsome, and completely ready to celebrate your brothers' nuptials."

"They'll only get married the once, as will I." He slowly lowered to one knee and took her hand in his. A delicious smile tugged at his lips and her heartbeat raced. "Cherub, we need to speak. You are the reason I live and breathe, the one woman I wish to share my life with, to raise a family with, and to share all your duties with. I wish to wed you right alongside my brothers as they speak their vows with their chosen ones, and I will feel completely bereft if I can't. I love you. Would you do me the great honor of becoming my wife?"

"Oh my." Tears misted her gaze as she dropped to her knees before him, her silk skirts billowing around her. "I love you too, with all my heart and soul, so aye, if you wish to wed this day then so do I."

"We'll never be separated again." With a hearty whoop, he stood and lifted her with him. He swung her about in his arms and kissed her, his delight and hunger for her blazing down their link. *"You'll be mine, in this time and every other."*

"Aye, as you'll be mine." She had her mate and she was never letting him go.

"Oh goodness." Megan stood inside Kirk's now open door with Michael right beside her.

"Well this looks interesting." Michael, dressed in navy pants and a tan shirt, grinned. "Sorry, we didn't mean to intrude but we heard voices and we just couldn't help but investigate what all the noise was about."

"Mum, Dad." Kirk wrapped one arm around Cherub's waist and opened his other arm for his parents. "Come and meet Cherub, my mate and soon-to-be wife."

Michael and Megan rushed across and hugged both her and Kirk.

Cherub couldn't keep her tears of happiness at bay. "We're getting married this day. So too are Iain and Isla, and Finlay and Arabel. We've come in order to take you back with us for the wedding celebrations to come, provided you wish to travel with us."

"Try holding us back." Michael arched a brow at her. "I've waited a long time for my sons to find their chosen ones." He clapped Kirk on the back. "Murdock's kept us well informed of all that's happened since you traveled into the past. Congratulations on finding your mate."

"I enjoyed every moment of the chase."

"I'm sure you did." Michael kissed Cherub's cheek. "Welcome to the family, Cherub. Your duty to our clan has always stood firm even though you've remained out of our sight and as much a legend as ever. Glad I am to see you chose to accept the bond with Kirk. He'll never leave your side, only aid you however he can."

"Aye, as he has told me and as I now know he too will."

"I love a wedding, and seeing all three of my sons speaking their vows will be a most magical moment." Megan jiggled about in her red ankle-length skirt and white blouse embroidered with red roses along the scooped neckline. "Cherub, since the moment Murdock told us of your bond forming with Kirk, I'd hoped with all my heart for this very outcome. It'll be wonderful to have a compeller, a fire-wielder, and a time-walker for daughters. When do we leave?"

"Right now, but first we must collect Murdock on our way."

"One second." Kirk nabbed his case, swept one arm around her waist as he breezed in behind her then eyed his parents. "You both need to hold onto Cherub. If you're connected to her in some way then you won't be sent freefalling through the vortex."

They all held onto her and she opened a vortex with Murdock's location in mind.

The dark ensued and moments later they arrived in a swirl of wind inside Murdock's solar on the second floor of Matheson Castle.

"About time you all got here." Grinning, Murdock rose from a forest-green couch underneath a wall-hanging of a stunning black and white drawing of this very castle as it had stood in the twelve-hundreds, Gilleoin's castle. Attired in his belted plaid, Murdock clasped the shoulder of a man wearing beige pants and a sword as he rose from the couch to stand next to him. "Cherub, meet Daniel. I had a vision this morning that showed me this coming celebration was about to unfold. I mentioned it to Daniel. Neither of us wish to miss this event."

"'Tis lovely to meet you, Daniel. You're most welcome to join us."

"Daniel, it's good to see you again." Kirk shook the man's hand then Murdock's. *"Daniel and Isla were partners, both working the same cases together and although not siblings, they're still as close as any brother and sister could be. Isla will be thrilled to see him, although Iain not so much."*

"It appears there might be a story there."

"There is, one I'll tell you soon."

"I cannae wait to hear it, although right now we must be away." Cherub held out an arm for Murdock and Daniel. "You both need to hold on to me while we travel."

With everyone connected to her, she opened a portal and sent them all whisking through time and into the past.

They whooshed into the great hall.

The trestle tables had been pushed to one side and up on the dais, Isla and Arabel sat in flowing gowns, Isla's cream with a rich entwining of cream and burgundy ribbons lacing the front bodice, and Arabel's a rich red with yellow lace trim around the hem. They both looked so stunning, and stunned.

"Dad." Isla squealed, grasped her skirts and rushed across. Murdock swept her into his arms and Isla cried out with excitement then clutched Daniel to her. "I'm so happy you're both here."

"Cherub wished for you and Arabel too to enjoy a surprise." Murdock motioned toward Cherub. "There are also to be three weddings this day. Kirk and Cherub's as well."

"That's perfect." Isla beamed. "Nothing could make me happier than to stand by both Arabel and Cherub as we wed our men."

Megan grasped Arabel's hands. "Welcome to the family, my dear. I'm Finlay's mother, Megan."

"'Tis wonderful to meet you." Arabel hugged Finlay's parents.

"Mum? Dad?" Iain stood at the front door in black pants and a dark tunic, his confused gaze moving from his mother to his father. "Am I imagining this? Or are you both really here?"

"My father's here too." Isla bounded into Iain's arms and he swung her around. "We're getting married today, you and me, Finlay and Arabel, and Kirk and Cherub."

Finlay jogged in and stopped and stared. "Whoa. I turn my back for ten minutes and look what happens."

Arabel giggled and skipped to Finlay's side. "Are you ready to flirt with a little more fire, my mate? 'Tis time for us to speak vows afore a clergyman."

"Always, my sweet. Bring on the fire." He pulled her into his arms and kissed her. "I can't wait to marry you proper. No more handfast wife, but a wife in complete and full truth."

"Then you will all need me if there are to be three weddings this day." Father John from the priory walked toward them in his brown robes and roped tie at his waist.

Nessa and Gilleoin, and a flurry of their clansmen, spilled into the hall. All cheered as they encircled them.

Kirk held Cherub's hands in his and gazed into her eyes. "This day I shall wed the woman I love. Thank you for bringing us all together so we could celebrate as one."

"This is another advantage to being mated to a time-walker. I shall always bring you and your kin together, whenever it is needed." She reached up on her toes and kissed him. "I love you, with all my heart. Thank you for hunting me down. Your chase has been the most memorable one of my life."

"I'll never cease hunting or chasing you."

"On that note"—Father John cleared his throat—"'tis clearly time to begin."

Cherub smiled. "Aye, please, go ahead, Father John."

They all spoke their vows, Isla and Iain first, then Arabel and Finlay, then lastly her and Kirk.

Applause abounded as they all sealed their vows with a kiss.

Cherub clung to Kirk as joy unlike any she'd ever experienced before filled her and overflowed her heart. She'd committed herself to her mate in all ways and he'd done the same with her. This day would mark the beginning of the rest of their lives, a most wondrous joining she'd forever cherish. Giggling, she kissed her new husband again and tasted heaven and all the promises it could bring.

Aye, after more than a thousand years of living alone, her life had now finally begun.

'Twas time to let love reign, and for her to share her duty with the man who held the other half of her soul, just as she held the other half of his.

I hope you enjoyed Kirk and Cherub's adventure-filled story. Don't miss the continuation of this series with *Highlander's Kiss*. The 'power of three' and their mates will be back to work some faerie magic amongst their kind.

Author's Note

Clan Matheson descends from a twelfth century man called Gilleoin, a man who was believed to have been from the ancient Royal House of Lorne. The name Matheson has been attributed to the Gaelic words Mic Mhathghamhuim which means "Son of the Bear," and the clan chief's arms carry two bears as supporters. In the twelfth century, clan Matheson settled around the area of Loch Alsh, Loch Carron, and Kintail, and gave their allegiance to clan MacDonald whose chiefs were the Lords of the Isles. Clan Matheson became a large and powerful clan with a force of around two-thousand men, although by the middle of the sixteenth century they'd diminished greatly in size and influence due to the blood feuds raging across the isles at that time. This warring left them to possess less than a third of the original Matheson property on Loch Alsh.

Interestingly, the other main branch of clan Matheson lived near Loch Shin, Sutherland, at this time, and it was when I discovered this piece of vital information that the story I wished to tell of this once mighty clan and the whispers in ancient times of their ability to shift into the form of the bear became clear.

For the purposes of this story, I chose for Gilleoin to have two sons, both when they came of age forced to go their separate ways, one remaining at Loch Alsh and the other traveling farther afield to an area near Loch Shin. Those sons would then lead their own clans, yet would one day once again merge to bring the legend surrounding clan Matheson back to life. It's time for the whispers to reignite. Clan Matheson are the "Son of the Bear."

This story is woven with as much accuracy to the period and locations as possible, although any mistakes made are mine alone.

This book forms part of *The Matheson Brothers* series, and each story within it is stand-alone.

Please feel free to search for any of my other works. I simply adore strong heroines, and have a ton of fun matching them with their honorable alpha heroes.

**Also available in paperback
Scottish Historical Romance**

Traveling through time…for a Highlander.

Highlander Heat Series

Highlander's Castle, Book One

Highlander's Magic, Book Two

Highlander's Charm, Book Three

Highlander's Guardian, Book Four

Highlander's Faerie, Book Five

Highlander's Champion, Book Six

by Joanne Wadsworth

Looking for more sexy Scottish adventure?

Read on to catch a preview of the next book in
The Matheson Brothers series.

Highlander's Kiss

The Matheson Brothers, Book Four

by Joanne Wadsworth

Highlander's Kiss

The Matheson Brothers, Book Four

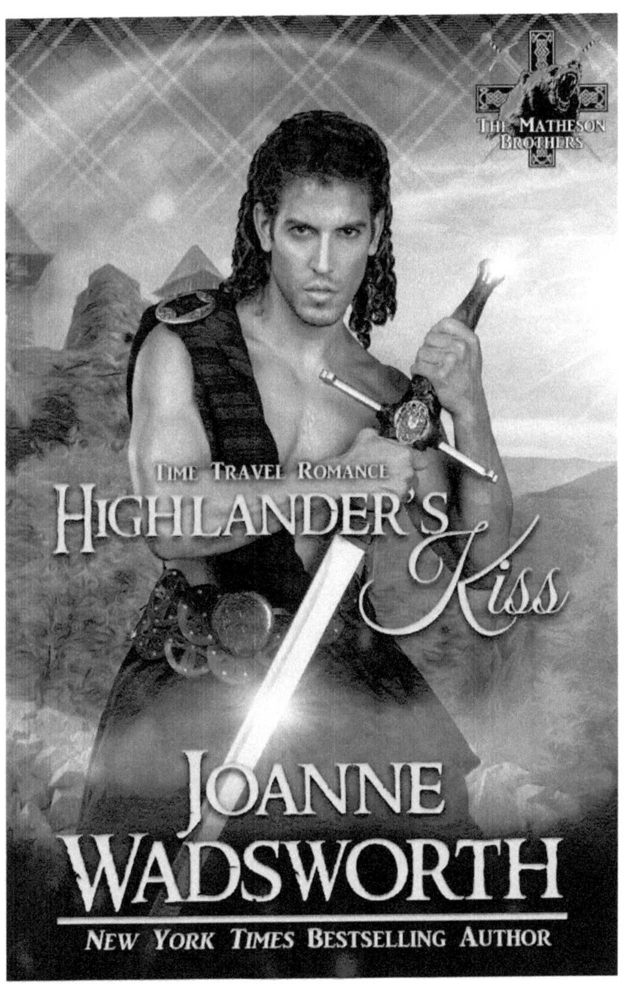

Gilleoin – The Legend

In the twelfth century, a man named Gilleoin became the first and only known man to hold bear shifter blood, an ability gifted to him by The Most High One. His clan was called Matheson, and when he mated with a woman carrying faerie blood, they created a line shrouded in secrecy, a line that far into the future, now neared extinction…

Cherub – The Fae Angel of Love

The ancient House of Clan Matheson, led by Gilleoin, the Chief of Matheson, Scotland, 1210.

Cherub dashed out from under the high arch over the front door of the castle and into the inner courtyard. She twirled around, her gown of white silk billowing in the wind whipping around her, the golden ribbons at her waist rippling and tangling around her hands. Arms raised, she reached out with her fae senses and allowed the very wind itself to bring to her the secrets it held, as she'd done for over a thousand years.

As an immortal time-walker and the faerie king's daughter, her duty was to aid those of fae blood who walked this Earth and she did so by ensuring the newly soul bound were brought together across the centuries and no longer separated by time.

Kirk, her warrior soul bound mate, swept in behind her, his chest a delicious wall of heat at her back. Gently, he caught her hands, whirled her around to face him then dipped his head to hers. His beautiful golden shifter gaze devoured her. "My elusive imp, it appears you sense lost souls this night."

"I do, far into the future, within your own shifter clan."

"Who exactly?" His excitement thrummed along their

merged mind link to her.

"Tavish and Tor, your second cousins, although 'tis Tavish's need that strikes me the strongest." Tavish and Tor, brothers and identical twins, had recently sensed their mates on the last full moon, and now, once she brought them here into the same time as their chosen ones, their senses would rear even stronger. Their desire to find the other half of their soul would consume them.

"Tavish is committed to his kin and being on call as our clan doctor. His patients come first, Cherub."

"Aye, but he will stop at nothing to find his mate, to ensure he makes her his." She closed her eyes and searched for the lass Tavish's soul was bound to. There, the intricate golden thread that belonged to Tavish swirled toward Julia's soul, her dear friend and one of her fae kind right here in this time. Bringing Tavish and his chosen one together across this wide chasm that separated them would require a little of her mischievous fae intervention, but 'twas naught she wasn't up for. Aye, a mated male longed for the chase and part of his journey in finding his chosen one was in the hunt, one she'd ensure Tavish was given.

On her toes, she reached up and kissed her mate's stubbly chin. She and Kirk had completed the bond such a short time ago, but she couldn't imagine her life without him. The moment they'd joined together as one, she'd taken a piece of his soul into her keeping and from that moment on, he too had become an immortal as she was. Her mate would stand by her side, for now and for all time. The exquisiteness of all she'd been gifted made her giddy with need.

Cloaking them both and ensuring none could see them, she rubbed the entire length of her body against his, her heart and soul singing at the luscious contact. "What did I do to deserve you?"

"I could ask the same question. What did I do to deserve you? I was certainly granted my ultimate wish the day I found you." He seized her mouth with his, his desire hot and hard and so very needy, the very same as hers pulsed. "To the skies, my elusive imp. I wish to show you just how very much I love you."

With a swish of her fingers, she swept them upward toward the heavens and gave herself over to the depth of the bond they shared and the fierce love they held for each other.

Tomorrow, she'd ensure Tavish and Julia met. Tavish's coming hunt would be one of the most intriguing she ever set in motion and she grinned wickedly at the thought. What a journey they would have ahead of them. Of that she had no doubt.

Chapter 1

Near the ancient House of Clan Matheson, Scotland, 1210, the following day.

Julia bowed her head as she stood before her parents' memorial stone wedged high on the cliff top ocean trail between the castle and her people's fae village. A good hundred feet behind her, the sea crashed hard and sprayed high, while before her, the forest rose sure and strong, the tall pines swaying in the fierce wind that rushed across the choppy waves of Loch Alsh and swept up the sheer rock wall and over them. High above, gray clouds bubbled ominously and she shivered and drew her white shawl tighter around her shoulders. "I'm so sorry, Arabel." She clasped her sister's hand and faced her. "I didnae mean to drag you all the way out here on this miserable day, but I just couldnae come alone."

"Dinnae be sorry. I needed to come as much as you did." Her twin squeezed her fingers then rested her other hand on top of the craggy stone holding their parents' names chiseled into the front.

Aleck and Adair.
Beloved parents of Arabel and Julia.
Taken from us far too soon.
Our hearts are broken.

"Sometimes, I can sense they're close even though that cannae be." Julia's heart heaved. Her fae skill of aura reading rose and her senses cried out for the gentle hum she'd always heard when her parents were near. The silence of their lost auras tore at her, as did the weight of her guilt. "'Tis my fault they're no longer with us."

"Nay, you must cease saying such a thing." Arabel gripped her shoulders and frowned. "'Tis Colin MacKenzie's fault that they are dead, as well as his snake of a son. I wish we'd never set eyes on Colin or Jeremiah."

"As do I, yet 'tis I who misread Colin and Jeremiah's auras. Mother and Father would never have traveled without a guard to our enemy's lair if I'd seen and heard correctly." Unlike any other fae aura reader in her clan, she was the only one who could sense both one's true intentions by the color of their aura and also the supporting sound their aura made. Even her aunt who held the same skill couldn't pick up the clear and concise sound that fully confirmed what the one they focused on truly intended. Her stronger skill had never set her wrong before, until the day she'd met the MacKenzies.

"Father and Gilleoin both believed Colin MacKenzie wished for a marriage of alliance, that his word was the truth. We were allies at the time, no' at war as we currently are." The war between their clans this past year had grown bitterer and bloodier than ever since the kidnapping and slaughter of their parents. Arabel squeezed her shoulders. "The Chief of

MacKenzie is the one who killed them, and with his own hand no less.”

“But—”

“No buts are permitted. You arena to blame.” Determination flared in Arabel’s blue eyes and lit the golden sparks glittering around the edge. Her sister was her closest confidant, identical to her in every way except for their fae skills. Arabel was a fire-wielder and held one of the greatest of the battle skills.

Breathing out, Julia tried to shake off her current frustration, but no matter how many times her sister told her that their parents’ death wasn’t her fault, she still struggled to fully believe it. She too was at fault.

“Come, let’s discuss this no more and instead leave Mother and Father an orchid.” Arabel lowered to her knees before the stone and tugged her down beside her.

Tears burned behind Julia’s eyes as she carefully removed the marsh orchid from her gown’s pocket and placed the brilliant burst of fuchsia-pink against the rough gray stone. Father had always picked Mother one of these orchids every time he’d crossed the wetland farther along the loch, and Mother had always tucked the precious bud behind her ear or within her long braid. At least her parents had left this world together, a blessing since Mother would never have survived without Father for long. Theirs had been a soul bound match, the same as what Arabel now shared with Finlay. Her sister was most fortunate to have been gifted with such a bond.

Arabel touched the orchid’s velvety soft petals, her bright aura clouding over and emitting a soulfully sad tune that tugged at Julia’s heart. “We’ll never forget them, Julia, and one day we’ll make certain Colin MacKenzie pays for our parents’ unjust death. He cannae be allowed to slaughter innocent people and get away with it.”

She would ensure he paid for it too. Her own aura, usually a melding of rainbow colors, now held a mournful black haze. She ran her fingers over the colors flickering on her arms and upper body and settled it back down. She'd never allow the MacKenzie to take another of her kin's lives, would seek retribution, for both her and Arabel, somehow and some way. She rose to her feet and drew Arabel up along with her. Across the other side of the loch, several miles away and not visible from here, lay the MacKenzie's lair. White caps rode the heavy swell of the sea, the rising storm gaining in momentum, just as the storm of despair did which raged right in her heart.

"Oh." Arabel touched her head. "Finlay calls to me along our merged link." Finlay had recently arrived here from the future with his brothers, Iain and Kirk, the three identical warrior brothers known as the 'power of three.' Their arrival had fulfilled a prophecy Nessa had spoken over twenty years ago, and along with their fae skilled mates, they were a force to be reckoned with. Finlay had discovered Arabel was his chosen one, a match their mischievous Fae Angel of Love had instigated when she'd first opened a portal and brought the 'power of three' into their time.

Julia adored Finlay, considered him a wonderful new brother. From the moment her sister had joined with him, she'd witnessed the telltale sign of their auras tugging toward each other's, just as those who were soul bound did.

"You're not returning to the future already are you?" She'd miss her sister and Finlay terribly when it was time for them to return to Finlay's time. Aye, she'd struggle to survive the separation. Goodness. Just the thought of her sister soon leaving sent her dismal mood spiraling downhill even further.

"Nay, we'll be here for some time. Finlay gave Uncle Gilleoin his word he'd remain at the keep with Kirk to care for our clan while he traveled to Stirling." Gilleoin had been summoned to Stirling Castle by William, the King of Scots, and he'd left with his son and the seer of their clan, hers and Arabel's grandmother, Nessa. So too Iain and his mate, Isla, had traveled with them, the two so eager to see all that they could of this time while they were here.

"What does Finlay need?"

"He said Cherub would like to see you, that she's waiting at the sea-gate landing and would like us to return."

"I wonder what Cherub would like to see me about?" It must be important. Cherub wouldn't have asked her to come otherwise. The wind whipped Julia's long golden hair about her waist as she turned toward home and followed the curve of the bay to where the House of Clan Matheson rose like a sentinel, its massive gray stone turrets and towering walls topped with battlements and double the guardsmen roaming the ramparts. 'Twas her sanctuary, and that of her clan's as well. Never would she allow the MacKenzie to take their home from them.

Along the sea-gate landing next to two moored birlinns, Cherub stood with her hands raised to the sky, her cherry colored gown with its cinched bodice making her a bright beacon of color. The Fae Angel of Love controlled the *air* element, could halt the wind or send it churning if she so desired. She could also cloak her form and become unseen to another, or if she wished, so too she could become as one with the very air itself and take on a mist form.

"I'm no' sure, but we'd best be away since Cherub awaits." Arabel brushed her hands against her forest-green skirts then crossed to her horse and untethered it from a low tree branch.

Julia collected her own mare, mounted and with the reins in hand, slapped her knees into her animal's flanks and rode back toward home. Bent low over her mount, she rode beside her sister along the high trail veering steeply downward toward the bay.

Arabel arched a challenging brow at her. "Do you care for a race? It might help clear our minds."

"Always. Catch me if you can," she challenged right back.

Never one to allow her sister to win a race, Julia tucked herself tighter against her horse, her gown's cream skirts beating against her legs as she urged her mare faster and whizzed along the trail. Stones scattered along the gravelly track, flew over the cliff's verge and rapped down the rock face before disappearing into the churning, watery depths below.

"Cheat!" Arabel yelled and laughed and pushed her horse harder.

"How does one cheat when riding a horse?" She galloped down the trail and along the grassy verge of the loch and as she arrived at the sea-gate, a mere horse-head in front of Arabel, she slowed her mount and brought it to a halt. With her mare snorting frosty air, she rubbed its neck, tossed one leg over the saddle and—

"Julia, wait." Arabel shot a look at her foot. "Your shawl is—"

She couldn't halt her momentum, or free her slippered foot caught in the trailing ends of her shawl. She toppled over and went down, hard. She hit her head on the edge of the stone landing and black spots danced before her eyes. All went dark.

* * * *

"Julia, please, wake up." Arabel's voice floated over her. "Now."

"I'm—" Oh dear, her head thumped as if horses stampeded within.

"Do as your sister says." Soft hands fluttered over her temple. Cherub's.

She forced the darkness away and blinked her eyes open. Arabel and Cherub wavered into view, their faces awash with worry. "I'm all right, just a bit—Oooh, everything is swaying."

"Which means you arena all right at all. You're also bleeding, and rather profusely." Arabel gripped the hem of her forest-green skirts, exposed her shift underneath and tore a strip from the bottom of the ivory cotton. Carefully, Arabel wrapped the strip around her head and tied it off in a knot at the back. "This should help stem the blood flow until I can get you inside. You're going to need stitches, several of them."

"Nay, please, no stitches." She touched the bound cloth at the back, her fingers coming away wet with blood. "I hate stitches, and I hate even more how rough you are when you administer them."

"I'm no' rough. But stitches are stitches. One cannae halt the pain when taking needle and thread to one's self." Arabel patted her hand. "Although I promise to be as gentle as I possibly can."

"Ladies, wait a moment, there's another option." Cherub slid one arm under Julia's back and helped her sit up. "I know of a healer within my mate's clan. Tavish is known as a doctor in the twenty-first century and I've been to see him a time or two when I've had an injured kinsman who required far more aid than what a healer in this time can offer." Cherub looked into her eyes. "Julia, in the future there are great advancements in healing and Tavish can ensure your wound is stitched without you experiencing any pain whatsoever. If you wish, I can take you to him."

"You're going to take me to the future?" She would gladly take Cherub up on her offer for that reason alone. Seeing the time and place where Arabel would soon live with Finlay enticed her to no end. "I would love to go to Ivanson Castle."

"Then we shall." Cherub glanced at Arabel with a slightly impish tilt to her lips. "'Twill be best if I take just Julia since Finlay willnae appreciate it if I take you so far from his side, even if only for a little while."

"I'll remain but only if you promise to bring Julia back here as soon as you can." Arabel crawled to Julia's feet and unhooked her shawl still snagged around her slippered foot.

"I give you my word I will." With one arm wrapped around Julia's waist in support, Cherub aided her to her feet. "Julia, you're to hold on to me while we're traveling through the vortex I open. No letting go, otherwise you'll experience a far rougher journey than what is necessary."

"I understand. I'll hold tight." She'd never traveled through one of Cherub's portals. Eager, she gripped Cherub's arm.

"Be careful as you travel." Arabel stepped back, blew each of them a kiss.

"We will." Cherub swirled her fingers through the air and the wind rose and whipped all about. A portal opened and she and Cherub fell away into the churning abyss.

Stars whirled through the dark and lightning flashed. Excitement buzzed through Julia and she gasped at the sheer beauty of moving through both time and space. What an adventure. She'd gladly fall from her horse again just to experience this.

* * * *

Far in the future and on guard in the misty moonlight, Tavish Matheson patrolled the battlements of Ivanson Castle. All remained quiet beyond the curtain wall, the surveillance cameras mounted on the topmost corners of the ramparts capturing the stillness of the night and nothing more. Beyond their keep, the forest stretched for miles upon miles within the mountainous ranges of the Highlands, providing their shifter clan with the perfect level of isolation they needed from the rest of the world.

Deep within the woods, an owl hooted then a second joined the first's nightly call. He scanned the woods, his shifter sight alone allowing him to see so very well in the gloomy dark. Unease rolled through him and his bear pricked under his skin. Something was off, although he had no idea what.

"Anything interesting going on tonight, brother?" Tor strode toward him in his belted plaid and shirt, his golden shifter eyes bright in the near dark.

"Not a thing, although that alone is making me even more restless." The wind rose and fog swirled over the treetops. The brisk breeze lifted his black hair and plastered his white shirt against his chest. He palmed his belted sword resting snug at his side. "Are you here to take over?"

"Aye, I'm on watch until dawn."

"Good, then I might just go for a quick walk, let my bear have a wee stretch before I head to bed." He clapped Tor's shoulder as he walked past him then bounded down the stone stairs and jogged out the gate under the raised portcullis. Allowing his bear his release, might just help to settle him down.

More fog swirled, the wind rushing around him. Within the churning haze, two women suddenly appeared, one of them Cherub. He'd never mistake the Fae Angel of Love, not when she'd visited him a time or two along with the odd patient from far in the past. The lass she held onto with one arm around her waist staggered on her feet and clutched her head. Blood oozed through the ivory strip of cloth bound around her head. She must be another patient, and with her velvet gown of cream sweeping to the ground, its sleeves draping over the backs of her hands, quite clearly a lass from another time. Aye, her clothing was from centuries past.

"Tavish, there you are." Cherub waved out to him. Her creamy skin sparkled, the glimmer a physical attribute held only by the eldest child born within the ancient royal line of the fae. "My apologies, I lost my focus as I opened a portal and missed arriving in your medical rooms, although no' by far. I need your aid."

"What can I do to help you?"

"This is Julia. She's close kin, and took a nasty fall from her horse and wounded herself. Could you take a look at her injury?"

"Of course I can."

"You all right down there, Tavish?" Tor gripped the crenellation as he leaned over it, his black hair falling forward over his brow. His gaze darted to Cherub and he grinned.

"Welcome back, Cherub. So you're the one causing the air to stir."

"Evening, Tor. I brought Dr. Tavish a patient, a very important patient from Gilleoin's time." Cherub smiled at his brother. For so long Cherub had hidden her true self from their clan, preferring to remain cloaked on her visits due to her sparkly skin, but no more, not since she'd become mated to Kirk, one of their chief's three sons.

"Let's get the two of you inside and I'll see to this very important patient." Tavish went to scoop Julia up so she needn't walk but then stopped. She wasn't from his time, might find his actions far too forward. Instead, he offered her his arm.

"Thank you." Julia slid her trembling hand through the crook in his elbow and curled her fingers around his wrist, her touch so sweetly warm and making his bear stretch deep inside him, as if itching to get closer to her. That had never happened to him with a woman before.

He shook the thought off as Julia glanced all about, taking in the high curtain wall, the forest then the gravel driveway which led around to the back of the keep to a large parking area in the rear. "I take it this is your first time here?"

"It is, although I expected to see something…different. Particularly since I've traveled over eight-hundred years through time." She watched her feet with each unsteady step she made.

"Just wait until you get inside." He guided her across the stony ground. "You'll see 'different' then. That I promise you."

"Julia, you'll love seeing all that this time offers." Cherub led the way under the arch and into the bailey. "Like electricity and running water. I have a home in this time which is located not far from here at Angel Bay. I dearly miss being there when I flitter all about."

The brisk breeze rose, swirled Julia's scent around him, a sweet white rose fragrance that tickled his nose. She smelled so soft and feminine and he dragged in an even deeper breath to capture more of her elusive aroma. His bear fairly purred his pleasure from deep within.

Julia's gaze lifted to his, her blue eyes as stunning as a clear summer sky and holding glittering sparks of gold around the edges. "Did you say something? I heard a purr."

"That was my bear." Although how she'd heard his beast deep inside him was intriguing. He hadn't emitted any sound. Only he could hear his bear. "My other half likes how you smell, and so do I."

"You do?" Her cheeks flushed an adorable pink. "I sprinkle rose oil in my bath, ah, water." The pink bloomed even brighter as she lowered her gaze. "Goodness, I cannae believe I just said that."

"I'm rather glad you did." He halted in the middle of the bailey next to Cherub, right beside the center well with its swinging wooden pail and sweeping ivy.

"Oh dear, Kirk calls." Cherub touched her head. "There's another emergency. Our connection can cut in and out sometimes when we're separated by time so 'tis fortunate he could reach me as he has." She gripped Julia's hands. "I must go, but just know I'm leaving you in the best of hands. I trust Tavish. He's a wonderful doctor, so kind and caring."

"If you need to go, I understand."

"I'll return as soon as I can." Cherub patted his shoulder. "I expect you to take good care of my kin."

"I'll take the utmost care. You do what you need to. I'll keep Julia with me until you return."

"Of course you will. I would expect naught less." With a mischievous smile, Cherub backed away then twirled the air. She opened a vortex and as the wind rushed all about, she disappeared within the swirling dark.

"Cherub said you're close kin. How close?" He steered Julia toward the front door of the keep.

"My sister, Arabel, is Cherub's sister by marriage, so very

close."

"I've heard of a lass named Arabel. She's mated to Finlay, right?" Which meant her sister held the fire-wielder skill. Even though Finlay hadn't yet returned to this time, he'd heard all about what Arabel could do from Finlay's brother, Kirk, during his flying visits in and out with Cherub. "Iain, Finlay, and Kirk are my second cousins."

"Then 'tis a very small world indeed...or mayhap time." She smiled and swayed, grasped his arm firmer.

"Here, let me carry you. You're not stable on your feet yet."

"I'm truly—"

He scooped her up and she gasped and clutched his shirtfront.

"—fine."

"No, it's best I carry you. I wouldn't want you falling and hurting yourself again." Too bad about the protocols between times. He wanted to hold her. Up the front step, he bounded then upstairs and along the passageway of the second floor toward his well-lit medical rooms at the end. Once inside, he set Julia down on the white-sheeted medical bed positioned in the center of the room, washed up at the sink and pulled on a pair of surgical gloves. With a tray of utensils in hand, he walked in behind her and set the tray on the side table. "Head wounds can be dangerous, but I promise to take good care of you."

"Cherub trusts you, which means I trust you too." Her words warmed his heart and he smiled.

"Thank you. I don't intend to lose that trust." He picked up his scissors, carefully sliced the bloodied cloth away then gently separated her hair. The wound was long but thankfully not too deep. "Tell me all about yourself, Julia." He yearned to know more. "Everything about the past intrigues me, particularly your time when Gilleoin reigned as chief of our clan."

"I'm an aura reader and can sense another's true intentions by the color and the sound of their aura, and Gilleoin is my uncle, wed to my Aunt Sorcha."

"I've never met an aura reader before." But that went someway to explaining her earlier comment. She'd heard the sound of his bear's contentment. "What does my aura tell you?"

She glanced over her shoulder at him, her smile making his heart lose a beat. Those sweetly pink lips of hers with their perfect pout, enticed him, made him want a taste. "Your aura is a pure white with a tinge of sizzling red at the edge, just as Gilleoin's is. 'Tis a shifter's aura you have, but there is more. When I focus on you, I can hear a gentle purr and that tells me you and your bear are as one, that your other half is rather content right now."

His bear was certainly content, any and all restlessness he'd felt earlier having disappeared the moment she'd arrived. "Your assessment is absolutely correct. Where do you live when not buzzing through time with Cherub?"

"At the House of Clan Matheson on the shores of Loch Alsh." She rubbed her forehead and grimaced. "There is an ache and it worsens."

"Did you lose any awareness when you fell from your horse?" He'd give her medication for the headache, the moment he'd stitched her wound.

"How did you know I fell from my horse?"

"Cherub said so when you first arrived. Do you recall her saying so?" Her clear confusion likely came from her losing consciousness.

"I do now you've jogged my memory, and aye, I lost awareness, Dr. Tavish. My sister woke me from the dark."

"Call me Tavish. There's no need to stand on formality while you're here." He reached up and tugged the overhead light on its metal arm closer. Light blazed and Julia's eyes went wide as she ogled it.

"Oh my, you have light without fire."

"This light comes from a light bulb, and definitely no fire is needed. This is a form of the electricity Cherub mentioned before. Lower your chin if you can. I'd like to flush this wound and clean it well. I'm also going to numb the area too. The most you should feel is a slight pinch when the injection goes in then maybe the odd little tug as I stitch the edges together."

"What is an in-jec-tion?" She twisted her tongue around the foreign word as she touched her chin to her chest for him.

"Doctors in this time use different tools to aid us in healing our patients, and since I've no intention of allowing you to feel any pain, I'm going to use an injection with a numbing agent inside." He cleaned the wound then smeared each side with numbing gel to ensure she didn't even feel the needle going in. No pain at all was his ultimate goal.

"Tavish," she whispered his name, her voice so soft as she leaned back a little against him. "Did you know your name means twin?"

"Which I happen to be." Injection in. "Did you not see Tor on the battlements outside? He's the one who called out. We're identical." He threaded the needle and set to work stitching the wound. "He was pretty hard to miss."

"I'm afraid I only saw a dark shadow. My vision was still a little spotty at that time. Arabel isnae just my sister but also my twin. She's a whole five minutes older than me, and always reminding me of it."

"Tor's a whole five minutes younger than I am. I have no trouble reminding him of that either." He ran another quick check over her head for any sign of swelling but there was none. Keeping a close eye on her throughout the night though would be a necessity, and he wouldn't allow Cherub to take Julia away until at least the morning, that's if Cherub returned before then. Another stitch. "Twins actually run strongly in my shifter clan. More often than not two cubs are born at once, although Iain, Finlay, and Kirk are the first triplets we've had."

"Twins run strongly through my fae line as well." She

gripped the edge of the thin mattress either side of her, her knuckles going white. "I'm nervous. I've never been all that good at getting stitches and I fear the first one. 'Tis an awful kind of pain."

"There's no need to be nervous." He covered one of her hands with his and her grip relaxed under his touch. "I've already made the first stitch, as well as the second." He began the third stitch.

"You have?" She jerked her head upright and stared at the long length of thread that led from the back of her head to his hand. A smile lifted her lips. "Well, would you look at that. You are a very clever doctor indeed, with a most magical touch. Should I ever need stitches again, I am coming right back here to see you."

"Thank you, but I hope you'll never require stitches again. Look front and center for me."

"Of course. My apologies." She resumed the right position and he returned to his work, bringing each side of her wound nicely and neatly together. "Are you mated, Tavish?"

"As yet I'm not, although on the last full moon my senses arose just as the other unmated males in my clan's did since the 'power of three' was unveiled and the fae village saved." He inspected his stitches, five altogether, which would dissolve on their own in another six or seven days' time. "All done, Julia."

"Already?" She glanced at him with the sweetest smile. "I shall never forget your kindness. You have my most grateful thanks for your aid."

"And I shall never forget the aura reader who paid me a visit from the past." He dropped his utensils into the automated cleaning machine on the bench, collected a bottle of water from the small corner fridge then with two painkillers in hand, returned to her and held them out. "I want you to swallow these pills. They'll chase away any lingering pain and allow you to sleep with ease throughout the night. I'll also need you to sleep over so I can ensure all is well."

"I would like to stay longer, to see what else this time offers. What herb are these made of?" She accepted the pills and humming under her breath, rubbed them between her fingers.

"Those pills aren't actually made of herbs but a proven medication." He uncapped the bottle lid.

"Would you look at that." She nabbed the bottle from him, swirled the water within then fingered the notches on the rim. "How clever to put a top like this on the bottle. I see the cap can wind itself over the head of the spout through these ridges. What is this bottle made of?"

"Plastic, a manmade substance. Pop one of those pills on your tongue then scrape it to the back with your teeth. As soon as you've done that, take a sip of water and gulp the pill down, then repeat again with the second pill." Her questions and delight at seeing so many new things touched his heart. He'd love to show her around his home, take her to some of his favorite places and watch her excitement continue to grow and bloom.

She swallowed the pills.

"Would you like to bathe and wash the blood from your hair before I organize a place for you to sleep?"

"Am I allowed to bathe? Whenever I've had stitches in the past, my sister hasn't allowed me to get them wet."

"Just this once you may bathe, then you're to ensure your stitches remain dry for the next few days. I've actually used dissolving stitches, so there's no need for me to even physically remove them once your wound has healed."

"Then a chance to bathe would be most appreciated."

"Good. Come with me. I'll show you to my bathroom and get you sorted." He set his hands on her waist and lifted her off the bed then slowly set her down in front of him.

Wobbling, she grasped his shirtfront and leaned her forehead against his chest. "I still feel so woozy."

"Lean on me as often as you need to." He tucked a lock of

her wind tangled blond hair behind her ear then once she appeared steady on her feet, offered her his arm once more and guided her out the door and into his bedroom down the hallway. His four-poster bed took up half the large space, the remainder holding a blue swede settee and an armchair angled in front of a wide screen TV. His bathroom sat off to one side and he steered her across his room and through the door. Sandy colored tiles led to an open shower in the tiled corner, one without any glass sides. The shower curtain though could be pulled across if needed, although he rarely used it. The bathroom flooring was designed to funnel the water away into the sink hole.

Julia ogled the room and gasped as she sighted the massive mirror over top of the white marble vanity. "I can almost see my entire self in that looking glass. That is the largest one I've ever beheld."

"We call them mirrors in this time, and it is a beauty." He picked up the metal shower chair, set it in the center of the showering area then flicked the overhead fan on. It whirred and fluttered the white towels on the side rail. "Come here, Julia. Take a seat." She did and he lowered to a crouch, bringing them eye to eye. "I don't actually have a bath as such for you to bathe in, but instead I've got a shower in which you'll sit underneath. That is how you'll be able to bathe and wash up."

"I see." With one finger, she touched the button on his shirt then glanced at the ceiling above and each wall surrounding her. An intriguing look crossed her face. "And how does one shower inside a bathroom when there is no way for a shower of water to reach me?"

"Showers are a modern invention and it's best if I show you, rather than try to explain how they work." He removed her slippers and lobbed them toward the heated towel rail. There, they'd remain dry and out of the spray's reach. From the shower caddy, he handed her shampoo and a bar of soap. "Feel free to use anything in this room you might need. What's mine is now yours."

"Are you certain I need to be sitting right here to have this…ah…shower?"

"Very sure." He chuckled and popped a kiss on her forehead. "I've never met such a woman as you, and it feels like forever since I've had such an enjoyable conversation. Seeing your delight in all these new things reminds me of how lucky we are to live in this time with all our modern conveniences."

"I've never had such an interesting and enjoyable conversation either." She touched her forehead where he'd kissed her. "What do I do next?"

"You'll need to take your gown off to shower." She had a full-length shift on underneath, the top lacy edge of it showing along her neckline. "Will your shift cover you adequately? You can borrow a towel if not, but it's best I remain with you while you shower since you're not yet steady enough on your feet. The last thing I want you to do is fall and hit your head on these hard tiles."

"Aye, I usually swim in my shift when needed so it will cover me adequately, although I cannae reach the stays in the back of my gown. Could you aid me?" She set the shampoo and soap on the floor next to her chair, rose to her feet and gave him her back.

"Absolutely." He swept her long blond hair to one side and exposed the creamy length of her neck then with her gown's cream and gold ribbons in hand, he unlaced her stays. "There, all done."

"Thank you." She wriggled the loose fabric down over her hips and the cream velvet swished to the floor. She scooped it up and hung it on the wall hook then wavered in her step, pressed her hands to her knees and drew in a long breath. "Everything spins when I move too fast."

"Then take a seat. I set it there for you for that very reason." He led her back to the chair and she plopped onto it and eyes closed, slowly breathed in and out. He hunkered down, rested his hands on her knees and gently rubbed. "I promised Cherub I'd remain with you and I will. Also, with dizziness usually comes nausea. Let me know if you feel sick so I can give you some meds to ease your symptoms."

"There is no nausea, just dizziness." She opened her beautiful blue eyes with their glimmer of gold at the edge and covered his hands with hers. "'Tis so comforting to be near you. You make me feel quite at ease."

"It's comforting for me to be near you too." More so with each minute that passed. Gently, he turned one of her hands over, picked up the shampoo bottle and squeezed a dollop of apple scented shampoo into her palm. "This is shampoo, what we use to clean our hair."

"It smells delicious." With one finger, she swirled through the creamy colored mix then cupped the back of his head, drew him closer and buried her nose in his black locks. "Mmm, whenever I eat an apple, I shall now think about you and this very moment." She rubbed the shampoo in her hands and grinned as the mix bubbled up. "Show me how to shower."

This he couldn't wait for, to see her surprise at the sight of running water streaming from the shower head. With the nozzle unhooked from the slide rail, he flicked the lever on then with his hand under the spray, waited for it to hit just the right heat—nice and warm and not too hot.

"That is so fascinating." Julia scraped her chair closer and grasped his hand being hit by the spray. "'Tis like a waterfall of water, a heated waterfall."

"There are metal pipes that bring this water right through these walls into this very bathroom. When one turns the lever on, water flows, or when the lever is turned off, the water halts." He passed her the shower head. "You're to control where the water goes."

She turned the nozzle on herself and the spray hit her front and flattened the thin cloth to her body. Lifting it over her head, she laughed as water sluiced through her locks and down to her feet tucked under the chair. Her big blue eyes met his, the twinkle within making him catch his breath. Comforting didn't even begin to describe how he currently felt around her. Inspired, thrilled, at peace and bursting with happiness, did.

"Here, let me help you." He picked up the shampoo and squirted more into his palm since she'd washed what he'd given her away. From behind her, he gently worked the bubbles through her wet hair, the silky strands sliding so sensuously through his fingers.

"I feel like I'm in heaven. Thank you for taking such wonderful care of me." She tipped her head back farther and sighed with delight.

Transfixed, he couldn't take his gaze from her. Tiny dimples either side of her lush lips begged for his touch and her sheer exuberance warmed the inside of his heart.

She waved the shower head up and down her body until the wet cloth was plastered against each and every inch of her. Slim legs and shapely calves, soft hips and the roundness of her full breasts. Hell, even a heavenly tease of her pink nipples showed. His mouth watered and his bear fairly purred for more. Never had the sight of a woman ever caused such a staggering need to rear to glaring life within him, not once, not ever.

He took the shower head from her and rinsed the bubbles away.

Was it possible the Fae Angel of Love had brought his chosen one right to his doorstep? Never had he imagined meeting his mate like this. He mulled the thought over, although not for long. Everything about Julia captured and enticed him. There was only one woman for him, his soul bound mate and it was her. Of that he was certain.

His chosen one sat right before him, and his soul lifted and rejoiced.

* * * *

Warm water streamed through Julia's hair and with it eased the thumping in her head, or mayhap that was from the pills Tavish had given her. No matter which it had been, she'd never felt so relaxed and alive as she had in this moment. For so long she'd grieved for her parents, but this trip here into the future had relieved a little of the terrible burden she always carried.

Tavish leaned in behind her, touched his cheek to her cheek and whispered, "You're all done."

"Thank you." She reached back with one hand and cupped his stubbly jaw. Being near him soothed her, in a way she'd never experienced around a man before, and the red edging his pure white aura shimmered even brighter. So too the gentle purr emanating from him rose to a wickedly low rumble. She swiveled around on her chair, rested one hand on the metal back and used it to keep her balance as she stood. Goodness. Her shift was plastered to her. She plucked it away from her chest, swiped a drying cloth from the rail and wrapped it around her. Such fluffy white cotton. Never had she wrapped herself in such a decadent cloth before. She rubbed her cheek against it. Tiny loops had been woven into the weave that thickened the cloth and made it lusher. "What is this called?"

"A towel." His shifter eyes blazed with smoldering heat as he gazed at her. "Feeling warmer?"

"Very." Heat flushed through her and she swayed.

"Hold onto me if you feel faint."

"I cannae halt this dizziness." Leaning against him, she nestled her cheek against his chest, his white shirt damp and clinging to his skin from the shower water she must have accidentally sprayed him with. "I wouldnae mind that bed to rest in now."

"I'll grab you something to sleep in first. I don't have any women's clothing in my wardrobe and I'd rather not wake one of the ladies in the keep to procure what you'll need, but I could offer you a shirt, some sweatpants as well."

The thought of wearing his clothing sent tantalizing thoughts swirling through her mind. She probably should say no and don her gown again, but any form of refusal wouldn't leave her mouth. "I'd like that."

"My clothing it is then." He disappeared out the door into his bedchamber, those dark trews he wore hugging his tight backside, a backside she truly shouldn't be admiring quite the way she was. Knocking her head had certainly scattered her usually good thoughts.

She shuffled about within the thick cloth, shoved her arms out of her soggy shift and tugged it down. The ivory linen fell in a wet plop to the floor and she stepped out of it, the towel still well secured around her.

"Here you go." Tavish returned with a bundle of clothing in hand, a royal blue shirt and men's trews, or what he'd called sweatpants. He scooped up her shift from the floor, wrung the water from it then laid it over top of the rail before he slipped back out the door and closed it after himself.

Against the wall, she leaned, dropped the towel completely and pulled his shirt over her head. The soft linen flapped down to her knees. She rolled the sleeves up to her elbows then tugged her wet hair out from underneath the collar and used the towel to dry it.

"Are you almost done?" His voice floated to her through the thick paneling of wood.

"One moment." She flapped out his gray sweatpants and stepped into them although they slithered right back down her legs and fell in a soft puddle. She stepped out of them and picked them up. "The sweatpants are too big."

"Let me see." He stepped inside and eyed them in her hands. "I might have a smaller pair, one that shrunk in the wash not long ago."

"Nay, this shirt will do." 'Twas decent enough with only

her calves and feet showing. She handed the pants to him, lifted the shirt collar over her nose and breathed in his warm and fresh scent trapped within the cloth. "I like your shirt."

"I like seeing it on you as well." He foraged in one of the drawers under the counter with its wide basin, nabbed a brush and gently detangled her locks before dropping the brush back in the drawer. With one hand at her back, he guided her into his chamber where the covers had been pulled back on one side of the bed. "Hop in. I want you to get as much rest as possible for what remains of the night."

"I'm to sleep in your bed?"

"I've used the settee before as a bed, and I'd rather you sleep right here where I know you'll be comfortable and where I can keep a close eye on you. You took a nasty fall and I intend to wake you every hour or two to ensure all is well."

"Our clan healer does that too with warriors who've lost awareness during a battle. She fears they may no' wake in the morning, so to set her mind at ease, she stirs them often during the night." She eased under the covers and jiggled about on the thick mattress. "This bed is so soft and so big. There's no need for you to sleep on the settee if you wish, provided you can keep to the other side of this bed."

"Are you sure?" He toed off his boots, removed his sword belt and propped his weapon against the wall.

"I dinnae mind at all." She pulled the covers back on the other side and wriggled back to make more room for him. He slid into the bed fully clothed then reached up behind him on the wall and flicked a switch which turned the overhead light off and plunged the chamber into near darkness. Only a shimmer of the moon's glow trickled in through a gap in his navy curtains. The gentle moonbeams played over his high cheeks and firm jaw. "I hope Cherub takes her time in returning. I would dearly love to see more of your keep and these fascinating things of your time."

On his side, he faced her. "When Cherub returns, I don't

intend to let you go, to just simply disappear back through time and never see you again." His aura flared and the gentle purr emanating from him rose to a low growl.

"I'm sorry." She rubbed his arm to soothe him and the growl tapered away. "I didnae mean to say something that would upset you."

"I'm not upset."

"Aye, you were. Your aura told me so." One's aura never lied, other than for Colin and Jeremiah MacKenzie's auras. Theirs lied with a lethalness that could kill.

"I just don't care for the thought of you leaving. That's all."

"I can ask Cherub if she will bring me back to visit. Since Arabel will be living here and our parents—" Her gaze misted and she blinked the hot rush of tears away. "Never mind."

"No, tell me what you were just thinking that upset you."

"My thoughts have dwelled on my parents a great deal this day. They passed away and now my sister is all I have."

"I'm so sorry for your loss." He curled his hand over her hip, his fingers warm and soothing. He tugged her closer, his gaze intent. "Do you want to talk about them?"

"I miss them, terribly."

"What are their names?"

"Aleck and Adair." Talking might help. "My father was a great warrior who held fae blood and my mother had the most caring heart. She studied herbs and aided our healer when needed. Both came from the fae village."

"How did they pass? If you don't mind me asking." He stroked her hip and she wriggled closer at his gentle touch.

"No' long after Arabel and I came of age, the Chief of MacKenzie requested a meeting with Gilleoin and my father. He wished to enter into negotiations for the marriage of his son, Jeremiah, to one of Gilleoin's nieces since Gilleoin had no daughters. That marriage was to be between Jeremiah and me. At the time our two clans were no' yet at war as we currently are."

She covered his hand with hers. She couldn't halt her need to share even more. "Unfortunately that meeting was just a ruse. I sat in on it at my father's request in order to keep an eye on Colin and Jeremiah MacKenzie's auras. They lied, which I didnae pick up on, and in doing so I misread their true intentions."

"What happened next?"

"Later that week, as soon as my parents arrived at Colin MacKenzie's keep to complete the negotiations, he had them tossed into the dungeon and then a demand sent to Gilleoin. My uncle was told to hand over his lands on the tip of Loch Alsh and in return the MacKenzie would release my parents. Of course many demands volleyed back and forth between them, and for several months until it became clear to Gilleoin that the MacKenzie was unable to listen to reason. That's when my uncle set out for their stronghold with an elite contingency of his warriors. Gilleoin's intention was to sneak in under the cover of darkness, rescue my parents and then return with them, but instead he discovered they'd been slain at the MacKenzie's own hand, several months prior and afore the first demand had even been sent. Gilleoin was furious and attacked. When he left, 'twas with a bloody trail in his wake."

"No one should have to lose their parents, and certainly not the way you and Arabel did."

"I would never wish what my sister and I have gone through on anyone." She plumped her pillow under her cheek. Her eyelids fluttered down and she pushed her eyes back open. All that had happened this day had tired her. "It has helped to speak to you of this." It truly had.

"I'm glad you've shared this with me." He tucked her closer, slid his hand right around her waist and palmed the lower curve of her back. "Go to sleep. I'll watch over you as you rest."

"Do you always watch over your patients with such dedicated care?"

"Always, but I shall be watching over you as if my very life depended on it."

"You are so very kind and caring, exactly as Cherub said." She focused on his aura then hers. No tugging.

'Twas a shame their auras didn't move toward each other's, as those who were soul bound did. He would make a wonderful mate. Certainly, the woman he was soul bound to would be one lucky lass.

She closed her eyes and drifted.

The dark rose and took her swiftly away.

The Matheson Brothers

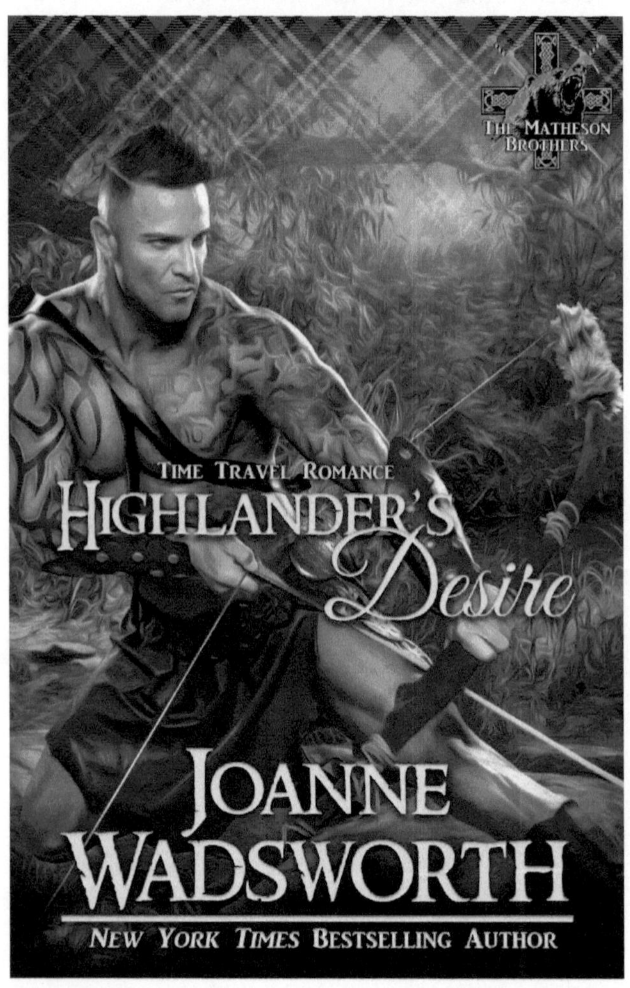

The Matheson Brothers Continued

Highlander's Kiss, Book Four
Highlander's Heart, Book Five
Highlander's Sword, Book Six

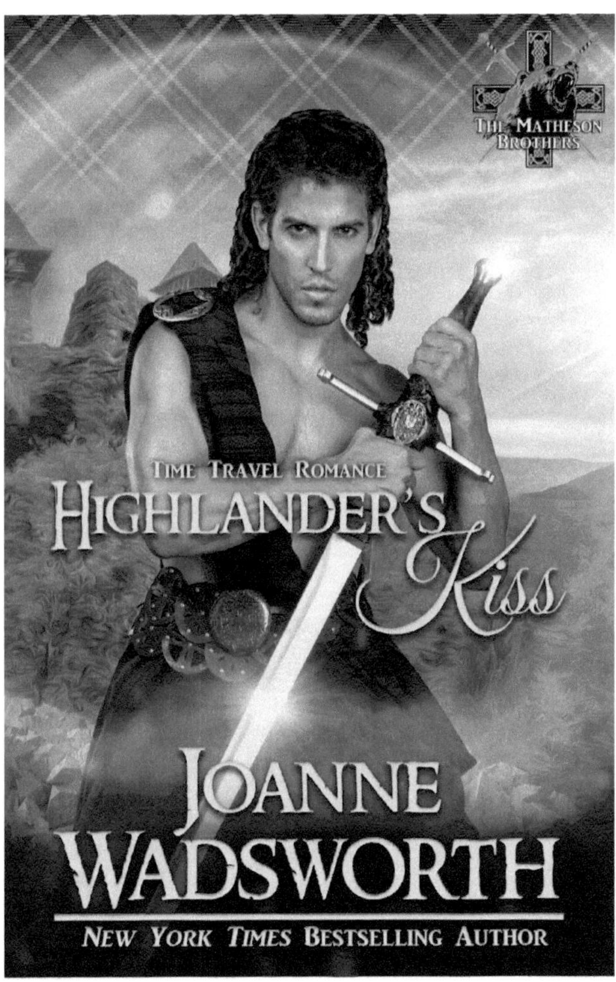

The Matheson Brothers Continued

Highlander's Bride, Book Seven
Highlander's Caress, Book Eight
Highlander's Touch, Book Nine

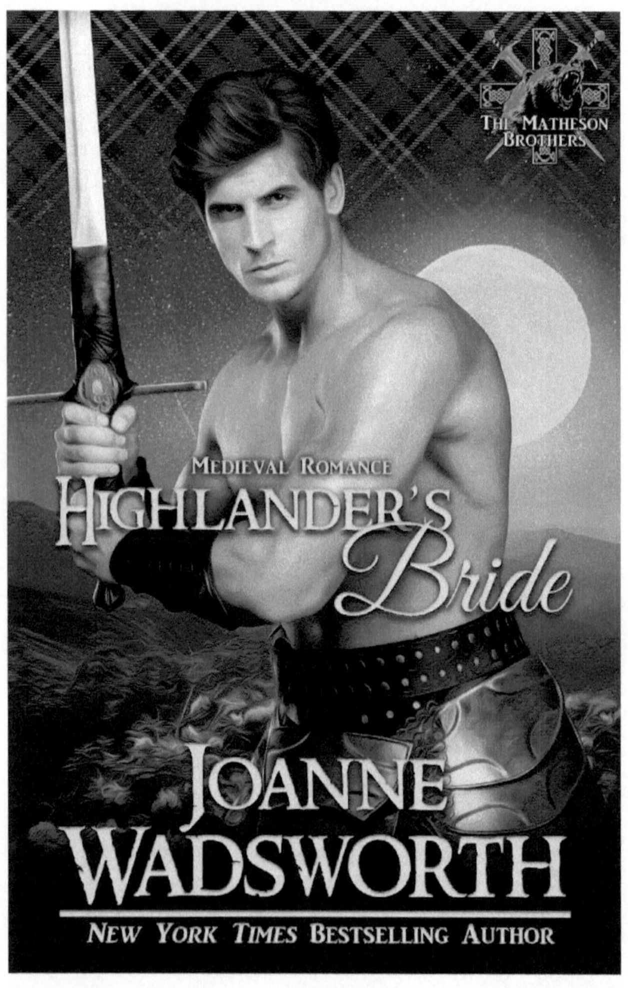

The Matheson Brothers Continued

Highlander's Shifter, Book Ten
Highlander's Claim, Book Eleven
Highlander's Courage, Book Twelve
Highlander's Mermaid, Book Thirteen

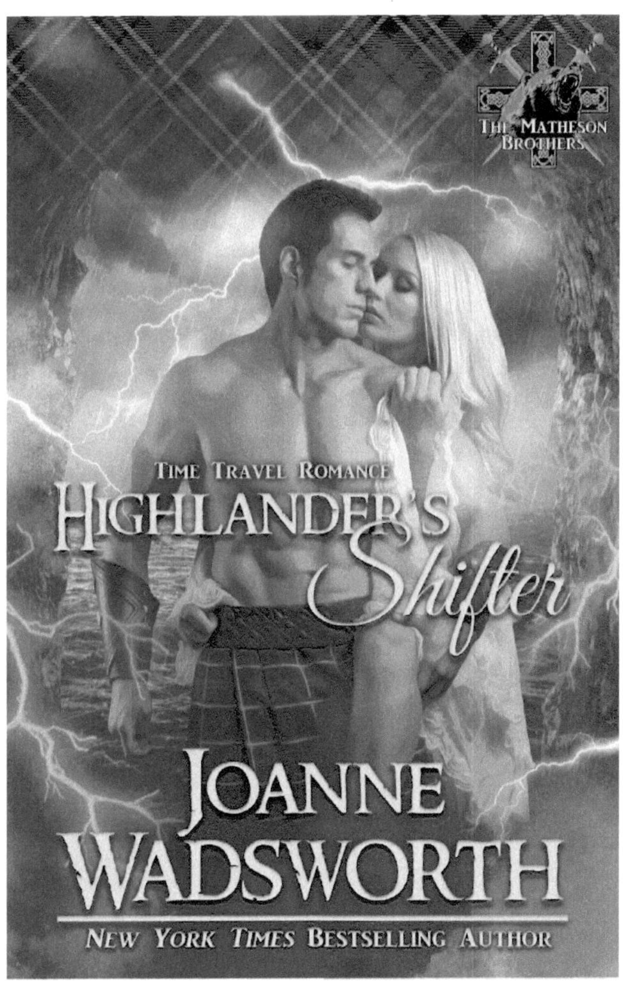

JOANNE WADSWORTH

Highlander Heat

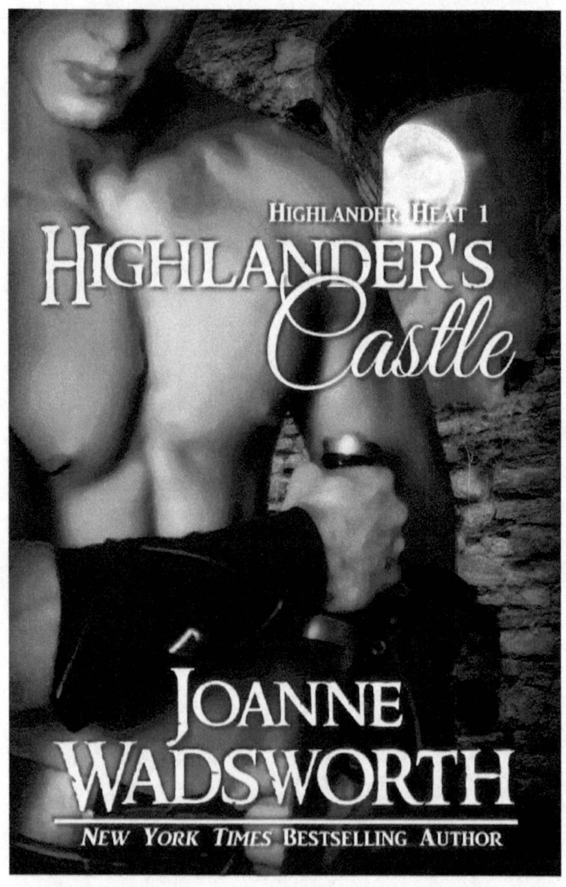

Regency Brides

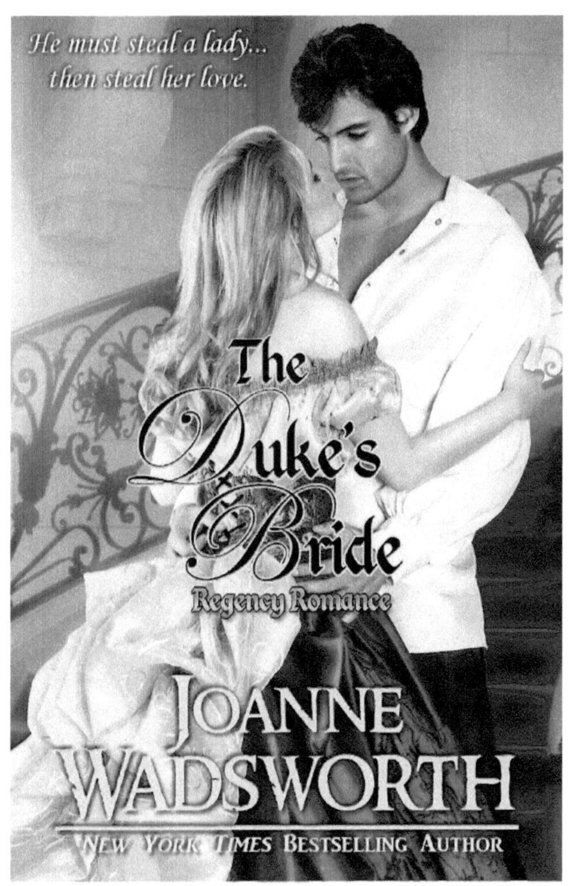

Billionaire Bodyguards

Billionaire Bodyguard Attraction, Book One
Billionaire Bodyguard Boss, Book Two
Billionaire Bodyguard Fling, Book Three

JOANNE WADSWORTH

Joanne Wadsworth is a *New York Times* and *USA Today* Bestselling Author who adores getting lost in the world of romance, no matter what era in time that might be. Hot alpha Highlanders hound her, demanding their stories are told and she's devoted to ensuring they meet their match, whether that be with a feisty lass from the present or far in the past.

Living on a tiny island at the bottom of the world, she calls New Zealand home. Big-dreamer, hoarder of chocolate, and addicted to juicy watermelons since the age of five, she chases after her four energetic children and has her own hunky hubby on the side.

So come and join in all the fun, because this kiwi girl promises to give you her "Hot-Highlander" oath, to bring you a heart-pounding, sexy adventure from the moment you turn the first page. This is where romance meets fantasy and adventure...

To learn more about Joanne and her works, visit
http://www.joannewadsworth.com

9 781990 034336